Discarded
Canadian Historical Mysteries
— Manitoba

Nancy M Bell

Print ISBNs
Amazon print 9780228626817
BWL Print 9780228626824
Ingram Spark 9780228626831
Barnes & Noble 9780228626848

Canadian Historical Mysteries

Rum Bullets and Cod Fish - Nova Scotia

Sleuthing the Klondike – Yukon

Who Buried Sarah- New Brunswick

The Flying Dutchman – British Columbia

Bad Omen - Nunavut

Spectral Evidence – Newfoundland

The Seance Murders – Saskatchewan

The Canoe Brigade – Quebec

Discarded – Manitoba

Twice Hung - Prince Edward Island

Jessie James' Gold – Ontario

A Killer Whisky – Alberta

Dedication

For the women history has forgotten.
I honour the role they played in creating
this great country
we call Canada.

Acknowledgement

BWL Publishing acknowledges the Government of Canada and the Canada Book Fund for its financial support in creating the Canadian Historical Mysteries collection.

Funded by the Government of Canada | Canada

BWL Publishing acknowledges the Province of Alberta for their ongoing support through the Alberta Publisher's Cultural Industry Operating Grant.

Alberta Government

Table of Contents

Chapter One

"Marguerite, you must go to him. Ètienne needs medicine, the fever is eating him up," Marie Anne urged her sister.

The younger woman shook her head, wringing out a cloth in cold water to soothe her child. "How can I? The English woman, she is there now, I doubt Miles will even speak to me."

"He must, Ètienne is his son!" Marie-Anne insisted.

"No longer." The words were bitter. "He has disowned the *bebes* and me, discarded us like so much offal. Now that his fancy *English lady* has arrived."

"Still, Marguerite, you must go and ask. I will come with you. Together we will convince your Miles to either send the British doctor or give us money for the medicine." Anne Marie pulled the dripping cloth from Marguerite's hand and threw it on the pounded earth floor. "Look at him! You cannot just let him die. If you won't go yourself, I will go in your stead."

Marie-Anne whirled around, grabbing two thick shawls from the back of a chair, and wrapping them around her shoulders. She planted her hands on her hips and glared at her sister. "Are you coming?"

"Yes, *oui*, of course. I know you are right. It is just my pride that stops me. For how long was I his wife in every sense of the word? If not for me, and you, and others like us, those soft Englishmen would never have survived their first winter. It was our relatives who brought them buffalo and other provisions to see them through, and us who cared for them, chopped wood, carried the water, bore their children..." Marguerite broke off, her throat closing in frustration and sorrow for all that they'd lost. Angrily, she swiped the moisture from her cheeks and straightened her back. "Come, we go. Alexandre! Come watch your brother while I go to your papa to ask for help."

The older boy poked the dying fire one more time before crossing the small room. He picked the sodden cloth up from the floor and wrung it out. After rinsing it with some water from the bucket by the bed, he wiped his little brother's face.

"*Maman*, he's burning up." Alex looked up at her. "Will Papa come and take him to the doctor? Why hasn't he come to see us lately?"

"Your papa will not be coming, nor will he take Ètienne to the doctor. The best we can hope for is that he will send the doctor or at least make provision for the apothecary to give me some medicine for him. I have tried the best I can with the willow bark, but it isn't enough."

"Will Ètienne die like Elizabeth?" Alex glanced at the empty cradle still sitting by the hearth.

"Not if I can help it," Anne Marie promised. She took Marguerite's arm and pulled her toward the door. "Put this on against the cold." She thrust a Hudson's Bay blanket into the other woman's arms.

"*Oui*, yes, we must go. You are right." Marguerite wrapped the woolen blanket tightly around her, and after one last look at her children, followed her sister out into the bitter wind blowing down the Red River, howling around the eaves of the small buildings and sending snow flying into their faces.

Alex's last words echoed in Marguerite's head as she shouldered her way against the wind. "Tell Papa I miss him." She snorted, as if Miles cared about them anymore. Even little Elizabeth, dead at six months of age, hadn't moved him to contribute to her burial. It was the English woman's fault. She was the one who turned Miles against them. Charlotte Windfield, what sort of name was Charlotte anyway? Grief stabbed her for a moment, not Windfield anymore, oh no. Miles married the *salope* in the church two weeks ago. So now she was Charlotte Ashmore. Lady Ashmore, the *pute*.

"Marguerite, come on, hurry up." Anne Marie looked over her shoulder and waited for her sister to catch up.

"Sorry, the wind is stealing my breath."

"Here, take my arm. It's only a little way more. Surely Miles will ask us in and let us get warm before we go on."

The walk from the Metis community to the more substantial homes of the British and Scottish population was a long one on a good day, for the two women walking into the teeth of the northwest wind it seemed interminable. Marguerite pulled Anne Marie to a halt in the lee of the church.

"A moment, I need to catch my breath," she said, also needing to strengthen her resolve not to do damage to either Lord Ashmore, her erstwhile husband, or the English *salope* now ensconced in the fancy house just up the street.

"A moment, then. But we mustn't waste time. Come." Anne Marie grasped her arm and towed her sister out of the lee of the building into the wind once more.

Marguerite led the way up the path to the front door, pausing before the two steps up to the porch to take a deep breath and straighten the blanket around her shoulders. Head held high, she mounted the steps and rapped loudly on the door. Anne Marie hovered at her side; shoulders hunched against the wind.

"Yes?" Lord Ashmore's man servant opened the door.

"I need to speak with Miles. Immediately." Marguerite blinked in the light spilling over the man's shoulder.

"I'm afraid that is impossible. You should know better than to come here where you are not welcome." He made disapproving noises with his tongue and made to shut the door, his strong London East End accent making it difficult for her to understand him.

"No!" Anne Marie thrust forward and stuck her foot in the door. "A child's life is at stake. We must speak with Lord Ashmore."

"Who is it, Gregory?" Light footsteps and the clicking of heels on the polished wooden floor preceded the voice.

"Nothing for you to worry about, m'am." He moved to block the woman's view of the porch.

"I need to speak with Miles," Marguerite shouted. "His son is very ill."

"Oh!" Charlotte Ashmore topped in her tracks and took a step back. "My husband has no son. I'm afraid you are mistaken. Now leave this place immediately."

"I assure you Miles does have a son, two of them in fact, and a dead infant daughter. Now let me speak to him," Marguerite insisted.

"Shut the door, Gregory," Lady Ashmore ordered, sniffing delicately through her nose before turning on her heel.

"Charlotte, who is at the door? For God's sake ask them in before you let all the heat out." Lord Ashmore strode down the entrance hall, tall and handsome with the lamp light gilding his blonde hair.

"It's no one, Miles. Just some beggars who have no business being here." She motioned Gregory to get the door shut. Now.

"Miles! It is Marguerite, Ètienne is sick to death. He needs a doctor and medicine if he is not to join Elizabeth in the church yard. You must help him." In her desperation, she shoved past the servant and the English woman.

"What in God's name are you doing here, woman? Have I not made it clear to you that you are not welcome here?" The Englishman's expression hardened.

"Ètienne," she repeated. "Ètienne is gravely ill. The fever is eating him up. Can you not ask the army doctor to come, *s'il vou plais*? He is your son, though you now seek to deny it."

Miles Ashmore glanced at his wife, aware of her distaste at this intrusion into their home. Not to mention her disgust for the Mètis woman currently pleading with him. Running a hand over his sleek hair, he looked down at the stubborn and resolute face.

"I cannot ask the doctor to go out on a night like this on such a trivial affair." He held up a hand to forestall her objection. "But I will have Gregory give you a note for the apothecary. Tell him what is wrong with the boy, and he will provide you with the necessary medicine. The note will assure him that I will cover the cost. But mark my words, do not come here again. For any reason." Taking Charlotte's arm, he turned, and they disappeared down the hallway.

"You must do something about that woman, she distresses me, and it is beyond embarrassing," Lady Ashmore's voice drifted back down the hall.

"No need to worry, darling. She won't bother us again. I promise." Miles glanced back over his shoulder; face twisted in a rictus of fury. The click of the door shutting cut off any further conversation.

"A moment then." Gregory all but shoved Marguerite out the door unto the porch. "Wait there, I will return with what you require as quickly as possible. In the meantime, stand out of the light. No need for the neighbors to have to look at the likes of you." He shut the door with a decisive snap, leaving the two women huddled together.

"He better not take too long, I'm like to freeze to death standing here," Anne Marie muttered, drawing the shawls tighter around her shoulders and cursing herself for not grabbing a buffalo robe instead of the woolen shawls before they left.

"As long as he brings that note," Marguerite said between chattering teeth.

"Here! Now begone." The door opened a mere crack, the note clutched in Gregory's hand fluttering in the wind.

"*Merci.*" Marguerite grabbed the folded paper, which was sealed with a blob of wax, before the wind could catch it and send it flying. The door slammed shut, the snick of the lock falling into place echoed in Marguerite's heart. Where was the man she had fallen in love with and borne his children? This man who was married to the Englishwoman was a stranger. Maybe she had never really known Miles Ashmore at all.

"Come, we must hurry. It's starting to snow again." Anne Marie nudged her sister, breaking her train of thoughts.

"*Oui*, we must get the medicine and get back. Poor Alexandre will be desperate with worry by now. I wish Guillaume was home, I worry that I ask too much of Alexandre, he is so young yet."

"Our brother should return from White Horse Plain in the next day or so. Alexandre will be fine until we can get home," Anne Marie dismissed her sister's concerns.

The two women hurried down the rutted street, headed for the cluster of buildings that formed the heart of the settlement. The Ashmore's dwelling was at the end of Fire Engine House Street and rather than take the colder windy road that ran by the river, the women trudged the length of the frozen road toward King Street. They kept to the side of the street that housed the Red River

Pioneer newspaper offices hoping to avoid the men hanging around the front of Monchamps Saloon.

Anne Marie clutched Marguerite's arm pulling her deeper into the shadows and away from the light and noise spilling from the doors of the saloon. Heads down, they scurried along as fast as they could manage.

"*Mon Dieu!*" Marguerite's breath hissed between her teeth.

"Come, hurry." Anne Marie tossed a quick glance over her shoulder at the brawl that spilled out of the saloon onto the street. "*Vite, vite*, before they notice us." She all but hauled her sister the remaining yards to the relative safety of King Street.

They paused to catch their breath before heading south past the dark surveyor's offices and the building that housed the Nor'Wester, the pride and joy of William Coldwell and his recent partner John Shultz. Schutlz's drug store was just past the Hudson Bay Company store but first they needed to get by O'Lone's Saloon. Slipping from shadow to shadow, Marguerite followed her sister, cringing at the sounds of revelry emanating from the drinking establishment.

"Eh!" She bumped into Anne Marie's back as her sister halted at the head of the lane opposite the saloon. "Why did you stop?"

"Well, well, what do we have here?" A rough hand shoved Anne Marie aside into the grasp of another man who materialized out of the gloom.

Marguerite drew herself up to her full height. "Let us pass," she demanded. "We are on an errand for Lord Ashmore."

"Sure ye are," the man holding Anne Marie jeered. He shoved her up against the wall of a nearby building, shoving her shawls aside while she struggled.

"I can prove it!" Marguerite's voice wavered and she swallowed hard. "I have a note from him, we must bring him some medicine for his English wife." She pulled the note from the waistband of her skirt and waved it at the man gripping her arm. "Let me go!"

"What's she jawin' about, Simon?" He lifted his head and grunted when Anne Marie attempted to knee him in the groin, the effort hampered by her skirts. "Leave off, bitch." He slapped the side of her head.

"Got a note, says it's from the English lord." Simon peered at the missive in the dim light. "It's sealed with some kinda mark. Might be she's tellin' the truth, Mark."

"Let us go," Marguerite demanded again. "Lord Ashmore is waiting for the medicine." She would have to go and take communion and ask God for absolution from her sin of lying of course, but if it got them out of this safely, she would gladly do so.

Simon broke the seal, the unfolded letter fluttering in the wind. "She wasn't lying, Mark. Note does say Schutlz is supposed to give these two some medicine. Let her go, we don't want to interfere with the Englishman's business. Won't go good for us if they don't show up back at the house." He glanced toward the saloon where a handful of men were gathered watching the encounter with interest.

"Was just lookin' for a bit of fun." Mark shoved Marie-Anne out of his way and joined his companion to peer at the note. "Hell, they're only Half-breed savages, ain't nobody gonna miss them if they was to disappear like."

Simon waved the note in Mark's face. "The Englishman'll miss 'em if they don't show up with what he sent them for. There's lots of women more willing than these two."

"I like a bit of a fight though, this one's more to my taste." Mark licked his lips and glanced back at Anne Marie.

Marguerite snatched the note from Simon's fingers and drew her sister to her side. "Come, we go."

The two women backed away from the men, who glared at them. "*Salope*!" Mark spit a stream of tobacco juice before turning his back and following his friend back to the saloon.

"*Mon Dieu*, my heart." Marguerite pressed a hand to chest, all the while hurrying her steps toward the bulk of the

Hudson's Bay Company store and the next corner where John Schultz's drug store sat just down from King Street. Heart hammering in her chest and sweating in spite of the frigid temperatures, she lifted her skirt and half-ran toward the light spilling from the apothecary's windows. Marie-Anne caught up with her at the doorway. They halted a moment to catch their breath before entering the establishment.

"What do the pair of you want?" John Schultz challenged them.

"I have a note from Lord Ashmore, medicine for a sick child."

Dr. Schultz glowered at Marguerite but stuck out his hand. She crossed the short distance to the counter and handed him the note.

"Seal's broken." He glared at her. "You steal this from someone? Wouldn't put nothing past the likes of you."

"No, *non*! It is for my son. Lord Ashmore gave it to me himself."

"We were stopped on our way here and a man opened it before he let us pass," Marie-Anne broke in. "You must recognize the lord's handwriting?"

Schultz took the paper nearer an oil lamp and squinted at the short note. Giving the women another harsh look, he exhaled loudly. "Looks alright, I suppose. But you can be sure I'll be checking with Lord Ashmore and if he don't make good for the medicine, I'll be a' lookin' for you two. Mark my words." Muttering under his breath, the doctor set out about concocting the medicine.

Marguerite shivered as the single pane window shuddered in the force of the storm, shifting from foot to foot. Finally, after what seemed like hours, Shultz slammed a brown bottle down on the counter.

"Take it and get out of my establishment, don't want any decent folks to see the likes of you in here."

Marguerite took a step back, intimidated by the fierceness of his expression.

"Thank you, *merci*." Marie-Anne scooped the bottle into her pocket and drew her sister out of the store.

"He looked like he wanted to murder us," Marguerite whispered, glancing back over her shoulder. "Why do the English and Scots hate us so much now? I don't understand."

"We don't need to understand, Marguerite. We only need to survive." Tucking her arm through her sister's Marie-Anne pulled her away from the door and into the wind. "We will go this way now, toward the river."

"But it's so much further than if we go the way we came," Marguerite objected, pulling free of her.

"Do you want to risk running into those men again? I certainly don't," Marie-Anne insisted.

Marguerite sighed and turned to follow her sister. "*Oui*, you are right, as always. We will go by the river." She hunched her shoulders against the cold. It was impossible to speak to each other without shouting once the women braved the full force of the wind. Marguerite glanced behind her, fingers of dread curling up her spine. It felt like someone was watching her, but who in their right mind would be out on a night like this in this deserted part of town? Someone up to no good, was her only thought.

"Is someone following us?" she shouted in her sister's ear.

"What? No, of course not." Anne-Maire paused and looked behind them. "Did you see something?"

"I don't think so, I just feel someone is watching us, following us. Perhaps those men..."

"Let us hurry then. I don't see anyone, but it is dark and with this wind you can't hear a thing."

The women strode as quickly as they could down the frozen dirt road, the sound of the river rising even over the roar of the wind. Almost there, Marguerite thought. Almost to the river road and then just a bit longer until they were home safe. There was no light here, only darkness and shadows. Reaching the lone building at the corner of the road, Marguerite turned her head toward the south and the road by the river.

"What are you doing? What is wrong?" Marguerite bumped into Marie-Anne who shied toward her suddenly. "Marie-Anne!" She grabbed her sister to keep her from falling, the woman a dead weight in her arms. A figure reared up out of the wind and darkness, she drew a breath to scream, still fighting to hold unto Marie-Anne. Then a flash of pain and darkness as she crumpled to the dirt still clutching her sister.

Chapter Two

Guillaume Mousseau pushed the door open and stepped into the cabin he shared with his family. His nephew, Alexandre was asleep leaning on the edge of the pallet where his little brother lay, a wet rag dangling from Alex's hand. Guillaume glanced around the dim interior, lit only by the fading fire. Where were Marguerite and Marie-Anne? It was very late, or very early, depending on your perspective he supposed. It wasn't like his sisters to leave the children unattended for any length of time.

Ètienne whimpered and thrashed in his sleep rousing Alexandre. "Hush, *mon frere. Maman* will return soon." He lifted his head and peered at Guillaume. "*Maman,* did you get it?"

"Get what, Alex?" Guillaume came and knelt by the two boys.

"The medicine. Ètienne is ill and *Maman* and auntie went to ask Papa for help."

Guillaume cursed under his breath. "When did they go?" He rested a hand on Ètienne's head. "*Mon Dieu,* he is burning up?"

"They went a long time ago. They should have been back by now." Alexandre got stiffly to his feet and went to attend to his necessary needs. "Why aren't they back yet?"

"I don't know. I will ask Fèlicitè to come and tend to Ètienne, then I will go to find your *maman* and auntie." He got to his feet and crossed the short distance to the door pulling it shut behind him. A few steps took him to the small cabin nearby where he banged on the door post before sticking his head in the door. "Fèlicitè?"

"Guillaume, you are back from the buffalo camp already. Marguerite said they weren't expecting you for a few more days. Come in, *entrè, entrè.*" The young woman smiled in welcome.

He stepped in and pulled the door shut behind him. "When did you see my sisters last?"

"Yesterday evening. Marie-Anne came over to see if I had any willow bark. Young Ètienne is gravely ill." She touched Guillaume's arm. "He is okay, yes? Nothing terrible has happened?"

"*Non*, he is ill but still with the living. Alex is with him, but I don't know where my sisters are. Alex tells me they went out late last night to ask Lord Ashmore to send the army surgeon." He snorted. "I don't know why she would expect that bastard to do anything."

"There is no more willow bark to be found right now. If the Hudson's Bay

Company has any, they are certainly hoarding it for their own people. The clerk told me yesterday that if more of us half-breeds would just die it would be a blessing to the community. *Le connard.* Marguerite was desperate for any medicine for the boy, especially so soon after the little one's death." Fèlicitè crossed herself at the thought of the six-month-old baby so recently buried in a shallow grave chipped out of the frozen earth.

"I just came home to find Alexandre alone with Ètienne. My sisters never returned after going in search of medicine for the boy." He scrubbed a rough hand over his bearded face. "*Merde.*" Straightening his shoulders and throwing off the exhaustion dragging at his bones, Guillaume turned to the door. "Can you look in on the boys for me until I can find the women?"

"*Oui*, of course. Go quickly, I hope nothing terrible has happened. There is so much unrest in the community now between the Canada Party and those of us who have been here the longest. I will do what I can for the child until you return." Fèlicitè banked the fire under the pot of soup hanging over it. She spoke to her mother to let her know where she was going, then turned back to Guillaume. "Go, go. Find your sisters." She shooed the tall man out the door.

Guillaume nodded his thanks and slipped out the door. He stopped at his own place to shove his head in the door.

"Alexandre, Fèlicitè is coming to help with Ètienne until I can return with your *maman* and auntie. Get some sleep, you look exhausted."

"*Oui, merci.* I will wait til she arrives before I lay down." The boy yawned wide enough to crack his jaw.

Smothering a grin, the older man stepped aside to let Fèlicitè enter. "My thanks again, Fèlicitè." He pulled the door shut behind her and headed toward the commercial centre of the Village of Winnipeg. His boot heels rang on the frozen ground. Where the hell were his sisters? They must have been detained, neither woman would have deserted a sick child. Someone must know where they were. Worry hastened his footsteps which brought him to Lord Ashmore's doorstep. Stamping his feet on the porch, he hammered on the door. "Ashmore! Open the door!" He waited an impatient moment before hammering again.

The door swung open, the Englishman's servant peered out, glowering at the uninvited person on his doorstep. "What is it that you want? Do stop the infernal racket, you will inconvenience Lord and Lady Ashmore."

"Where are my sisters?" he demanded, throttling down the urge to lift the officious little man up by his collar.

"Whom, pray tell, are your *sisters*?" Gregory invested the word sisters with as much distain as possible. "I can't imagine why you would come here looking for anyone."

Guillaume ground his teeth and forced himself to speak in a reasonable tone. "My sister, Marguerite, surely you remember her? I'm told she came here last night to ask Ashmore for help."

Gregory inhaled sharply through his nose. "Oh, those *women...*" he began, contempt dripping from his words.

"Yes, those women," Guillaume spit the words. "My sisters who made sure you and the Englishman survived your first three winters here, who nursed you when you fell ill. Where are they right now?" He took a step forward, looming over the smaller man.

Gregory's Adam's apple bobbed in his thin neck above the starched neck cloth tucked into his tailored coat. "I'm sure I don't know. It is hardly my job to keep track of the riff raff that abounds in this settlement."

Guillaume took another step that brought him beneath the lintel, the sound of a woman's voice halting his intention to strangle the man with his own stock.

"Gregory," the imperious voice preceded the rustle of skirts as the mistress of the house entered the hall, "what is all the noise about. And why are you standing with the door open? Oh!" She caught sight of Guillaume's imposing figure blocking the entry. Oh, it's you! What are you doing here?

Gregory, get this creature out of my doorway."

"Lady. Ashmore." Guillaume removed his hat and gave the woman a slight nod. "A pleasure."

She sniffed. "It certainly is not a pleasure, I assure you. Kindly remove your person from my presence." Charlotte Ashmore looked down her aristocratic nose at him and made slight shooing motions with her hands. "Gregory," she commanded, indicating the interloper with a nod of her perfectly coiffed head, remove this person. Now!"

"Not until I have the information I came for, ma'am. My sisters came here last night to see Lord Ashmore to request help for Ètienne, who is I might remind you, the lord's son as well as my sister's."

"How dare you insinuate such a thing!" Charlotte Ashmore gasped and blanched before the red tinge of temper rose up her throat and across her pale cheeks. "My husband has no children," she paused, "at least no legitimate children, which is to say, none that count."

"I assure you, madame, Ètienne and Alexandre do count very much, but if you would be so kind as to answer my question?" Guillaume held onto the reins of his temper with iron hands. "Did my sisters speak with your husband last evening?"

"Oh, very well. If it will get your person and your filthy boots off my doorstep," she wrinkled her nose in disgust and lifted a lavender scented lacy handkerchief daintily to her nose, "and away from here. Gregory, you may tell this *person* what you know." After, a last disdainful sniff, she turned and drifted down the hall, head held high, heels clicking on the floor.

"Well?" Guillaume glowered at the servant, hands clenched at his side.

"Very well since Her Ladyship insists. But it is more than you deserve. Yes, the women you refer to as your sisters, did indeed come here last evening asking to speak with His Lordship. He dealt with them and sent them on their way." He nodded as if this was sufficient information to send the man on his way.

"And?"

"And what?" Gregory stood his ground.

"Did Ashmore offer any help, when did they leave here? Something a bit more helpful, if you would."

"Oh very well." Gregory sighed and managed to look very put upon. "Your sisters came begging asking for the army surgeon to come out in the middle of the night to attend one of their offspring. Such nerve! My lord was kind enough to provide them with a note instructing Doctor Schultz to provide them with medicine for the child. Far kinder than he needed to be."

"At least he did that much. What time did the women leave here? It's important. They did not return home last night."

Gregory shrugged as if it was of no consequence. "I'm sure many women like them didn't come home last night."

"Be careful of what you say," Guillaume warned. "What time did they leave?"

"It was close to midnight, near as I can recall." The servant supplied the information grudgingly.

Guillaume gave a curt nod of thanks and stepped off the porch. It appeared Marguerite and Marie-Anne made it this far, so obviously their next stop would have been John Schultz's store. He turned his steps that way through the early morning foot traffic. A commotion caught his attention. A cluster of Company men and onlookers hurried toward the river, voices raised in excitement. Random words reached his ears. Bodies, bodies were discovered on the riverbank. *Merde*! It doesn't necessarily have anything to do with Marguerite and Marie-Anne, he told himself. But his stomach still clenched, and he broke into a run in order to catch up and join the men.

The group halted by the river and milled around, held back by the ring of men accompanying the Hudson Bay officers. Guillaume elbowed his way to the front, heedless of the feet he trod on. Reaching the wall of onlookers, he gripped the nearest man's arm.

"What have they found? Do you know who it is?" He peered over the shorter man's shoulder. A bit of ragged shawl fluttered in the brisk breeze. "Marie-Anne!" Guillaume shoved the man aside and shook off the next man who sought to hold him back. Pushing his way through, he approached the small group of Hudson's Bay officers surrounding the bodies.

"Hold, you!" One of the clerks moved to block his vision. "Get back where you belong!"

"Lord Ashmore! I demand to speak with Lord Ashmore!" Guillaume stood his ground.

"Yes, what is it?" Miles Ashmore turned from his perusal of the scene at his feet. "Ah, Mister Mousseau, what brings you here? This isn't a place for you."

"Don't you recognize her?" Guillaume shook off the man still attempting to hold him back and knelt by the figures on the cold earth. He pushed back the hank of hair that had come unbound and covered the nearest victim's face. It was Marie-Anne, he was sure of it because of the colourful shawls, though her features were beaten beyond recognition. He glared up at Ashmore. "This is my sister, Marie-Anne." He rose and turned the other woman over. "And this is also my sister, Marguerite." He surged to his feet, taking two long strides closer to the Englishman. "How did this happen? They came to you for help, how did they end up like this?"

"I'm sure I don't know." Lord Ashmore held up his hands, silently signalling the men to step back for the moment "I gave them a script to take to Doctor Schultz in order to obtain medicine for the boy. Other than that I have no idea where your women went afterward. It really is no concern of mine."

"No concern of yours?" Guillaume's voice dropped dangerously low. "Two women are murdered, one of them is the mother of your sons, and you claim it is no concern of yours?"

He ignored the surprised whispers from the enlisted men behind him, gaze pinning the man in his place. "Murders of innocent women are of no concern to you?" he repeated.

"I might quibble with the term innocent," Ashmore began before quickly changing tack when Guillaume's expression darkened, "but be that as it may, I think this is something that your community should handle. It's not really a matter for me to be concerned with." He stepped back, in effect washing his hands of the situation.

J.J. Hargreaves pushed his way through the line of soldiers. "What do we have here? Oh dear." He stopped at the sight of the battered women laying on the banks of the Red River. Hargreaves came to stand beside Mousseau. "Do you know who they are?" He pulled a note pad and graphite stick out of his pockets.

"*Oui,* my sisters," he said shortly.

"How did they come to be here so early in the morning, and in such condition?" Hargreaves licked the end of his pencil.

"I do not know. They came into the village late last night to ask for medicine for my nephew. They went to the lord's house and got a script for Doctor Schultz and somehow ended up here." He glared at Ashmore. "I came looking for them when I arrived home this morning and was informed they hadn't returned last night."

"Really?" Hargreaves scribbled on his note pad. "Did they ever make it to the apothecary's?"

"That I do not know, yet. I had only started my search when I heard the commotion and came here with no idea of what I would find. Certainly, not this." He nodded at his sisters' bodies.

"Of course." Hargreaves nodded, turning to speak to Lord Ashmore. "When did you become aware something was wrong?"

"At the same time as everybody else." The man's reply was terse.

"Who found the bodies, who reported it to you?" Hargreaves persisted.

Guillaume refused to be moved, intent on hearing Ashmore's response.

"A fur trader on his way to the Hudson's Bay store." He glanced at Guillaume. "One of *your* people."

"Who was it?" Mousseau demanded.

"How am I to know that? It was a fur trader, dirty and stinking. How am I to tell one from the other of you?"

Guillaume clenched his jaw. He would find out, someone at the store would know. The clerks loved gossip and surely this would be top of their minds this morning. First, he needed to take care of his sisters. "I need to find someone to help me move my sisters. Are you willing to have a few of your men stay here until I return with a cart and some help."

Ashmore's expression was undecided, glancing at the nearest men who were muttering among themselves, hunched against the cold.

"She is the mother of your sons, surely you can give her that much respect," Guillaume insisted.

The Englishman nodded, signalling for three of the Company men to stay with the bodies and ordering the others to move the group of onlookers away.

"Let no one touch them," Guillaume ordered the three men who met his words with blank faces. "No one."

"See that no one interferes with anything," Ashmore directed the men before marching off with the others trailing behind.

Hargreaves tagged along behind Guillaume as he strode toward the Nor-Westers offices where his friend Pierre worked for William Coldwell and John Schultz. There would most likely be a Red

River cart stored behind the building that he could borrow. Guillaume continued to ignore Hargreaves questions, repressing the almost overwhelming pang of loss. He let anger push his grief to the back of his mind, concentrating instead on first, the dignity of his sisters' remains, and then on avenging their senseless deaths. *Merde*, how was he to tell Alexandre, and even petite Ètienne, about their *maman* and auntie. The thought caused a falter in his steps and Hargreaves took the opportunity to pull him to a halt.

"Who do you think is responsible for the murders? Any ideas?" He paused when Guillaume shoved him aside and carried on toward his destination. "Your sister was involved with the English lord, wasn't she? You think he had anything to do with this?"

Guillaume halted abruptly and swung around, startling the reporter. "The English lord had best hope not. If I find anything linking him to my family's loss it will not go well for him." He brushed past the man again and left him standing in the roadway, scribbling in his note pad. Reaching the office of the Nor-Wester, Mousseau paused to take a breath before entering. Pierre was particularly fond of Marie-Anne, so he did not relish the thought of giving him the news he brought with him. Another moment to gather his resolve, then Guillaume pushed the door open and entered.

"Is Pierre about?" he enquired of Mr. Coldwell who was behind the counter.

"In the back, just a moment." He rose from his chair and called into the back room over the noise of the printing press. "Pierre! Someone to see you."

"Ah, Guillaume, *mon ami.* What brings you here so early?" Pierre came to the counter, wiping his hands on an ink-stained cloth. Catching sight of his friend's expression, he set the cloth down and came around the end of the counter. "What is it? What has happened?" He grasped his friend's arm. "I heard Ètienne was sick…"

"No, not Ètienne—"

The arrival of two men, flushed with excitement interrupted him.

"Did ya hear, did ya? Two murdered Frenchie half-breeds down by the river. Got three Company men guarding 'em. You gonna get this in the next paper."

Guillaume rounded on the two men. "Get out! Get out now!"

The braver of the two held up his hands. "No need to get angry, just reporting the news to the paper." The two men backed out the door.

"Guillaume?" Pierre drew his friend's attention from the retreating backs of the men. "Is it true. Who did they find?"

Mousseau swallowed the lump of anger and grief in his throat before meeting Pierre's gaze. "It is Marguerite and Marie-Anne." His voice faltered.

"*Mon Dieu.* Say it is not so." Pierre's face blanched and he gripped the counter for support. "Not Marie-Anne."

Guillaume moved to support his friend. "*Oui*, that is why I came here. To tell you and to ask for your help in moving them to a safe place and I suppose I must speak to Father Tachè."

"Of course, of course. What do you need?" Pierre regained control of his emotions with a visible effort.

"Your strong back and the loan of a cart to transport the bodies."

"Mister Coldwell," Pierre turned to his employer, "Can I please beg the use of the cart to help my friend?"

"Yes, of course. I couldn't help but overhear, my condolences."

"*Merci.*" Guillaume offered a curt nod of his head in thanks.

"Let me get my coat and hat." Pierre picked the articles off hooks by the door. "Come through this way, we can go out the back." He led the way around the counter and past the now silent printing press. The air sharp with the scent of ink and lead.

Guillaume followed in his wake, giving the massive press a wide berth. The machine hunkered like a huge beast which might leap from its bed at any moment. He breathed a sigh of relief when the door closed behind them, somewhat muffling the scent of ink and wet paper they left behind.

"The cart is here, do we need the horse to pull it or are we sufficient by ourselves?" Pierre lifted the shaft of the Red River cart to tug it forward a few inches.

"Perhaps we should use the horse. It will be quicker, and I still have to tell my nephews about what has happened. But first, I want to be sure my sisters are safe and away from prying eyes." He frowned. "And I want to take a good look at the place they were murdered. See if I can find anything that might give a clue to who did this to them."

Pierre moved off to bring the horse from its place in a lean to behind the building. Guillaume took the harness down from the pegs on the wall and threw them over the horse's back before they put the animal between the shafts. It took only minutes to fasten the buckles and tighten what needed tightening. Together, they got the beast hitched to the cart and set off, one on each side of the animal, the empty cart lumbering along behind them, jouncing over the frozen ruts.

Guillaume's heart twisted in his chest when the men guarding the site came into view. The realization of what lay there hit him anew, somehow in the mix of anger and anxiety to claim the bodies, he'd managed to bury the stark reality that his younger sisters were gone. He forced himself to keep walking though part of him wanted to run and hide somewhere to weep out his grief and sorrow. He let the anger come to the forefront again, straightening his shoulders.

"Jesu save us." Pierre crossed himself when the men parted to reveal the battered remains. He dropped to his knees beside Marie-Anne, gently pushing the hair back from her face.

The three Company men took their leave without acknowledging the two Mètis men. One of them hawked as he left. Rage leaped in Guillaume's chest, but he throttled it down. There were more important things to take care of than beating on a soldier which would only result in Guillaume languishing in jail. *Salouds! English Bastards.*

Pierre rose with Marie-Anne cradled in his arms. Tears shone on his cheeks. "Who would do such a thing? Why?" He laid her gently in the bed of the cart, smoothing down her skirts and arranging her hands over her shawls.

Guillaume knelt and gathered Marguerite up off the ground. Her fingers were clenched tightly. When he settled her beside her sister in the cart, he pried those fingers open. A silver button lay in her palm. "Look at this?" He called Pierre's attention to the button. "It must belong to whoever attacked them, perhaps."

"That would seem to be a good guess," Pierre agreed. "But who?"

"It is hard to say. Many men have silver buttons even some of the traders."

"Let's have a better look at where they were attacked." Pierre scrutinized the ground. He'd been an accomplished tracker before taking up the printing trade. Guillaume joined him. "Look here, the ground is scuffed over by this building." The men moved closer, careful to avoid stepping in the snow clustered by the walls. "Ha!" Pierre pointed to the imprint of boots in the snow at the side of the building. "They hid here and waited for them. But why Marguerite and Marie-Anne? They have nothing to do with any of the political upset that is going on. Nor do we, as far as I am aware." Pierre looked at Guillaume.

He shrugged. "While I do not support the Canada Party, I am not so deeply involved with Riel and his idea of a provisional government either. Perhaps they were just in the wrong place at the wrong time?" He scratched his beard.

Pierre continued to survey the area. He pointed out more scuff marks and then to the spot where dark blood lay congealed on the ground. "This is where they were killed," he stated calmly, although his heart raced, and grief was a physical pain in his chest.

Guillaume noted the scuff marks in the frozen ruts. "Why drag them to the river? If whoever did this was planning to dump them in, why stop at the riverbank?"

"Perhaps they were interrupted by someone or something?" Pierre pushed his hat back on his head. "We must ask around, perhaps someone saw something we should know about.”

“I agree.” Guillaume nodded and turned toward the cart. But for now, we need to get the women taken care of and inform the priest in St. Boniface. And I need to break the news to the little ones.” A glint of something by the riverbank caught the weak sunlight. “What is this?” Quick strides brought him to the edge of where the bodies were found. He knelt and used his knife to pry the object out of the frozen dirt and snow.

“What is it? What did you find?” Pierre looked over his shoulder as Guillaume rose and dropped the bit of metal into the palm of his leather glove.

“It’s a ring, a gold ring.” He turned it over with the point of his knife. “A signet ring, I think.”

“A woman’s ring? It’s not very large,” Pierre observed.

“Perhaps, but I suppose it could belong to a small man,” Mousseau responded.

“It might not belong to whoever did this. The ring could have been stolen before the women were attacked,” Pierre said. “Still, it is significant. It certainly doesn’t belong here.”

Guillaume tipped the ring into a pouch he kept at his waist, tucked into the embroidered sash he wore. “Between the ring and the button we have a place to start looking. I see no point in informing the Hudson Bay Company officials or anyone else about what we've found. It seems no one cares what happens to any of us so long as the British and Scots are left alone."

"Riel cares," Pierre protested. "He may be able to offer some assistance." Pierre took the horse's reins and set the cart in motion, the large wheels creaking in protest at the cold and the rutted road. Guillaume fell into step beside him.

"Yes, we need to get the women to Father Tachè at Fort Garry. He will see that they are kept well until we can arrange burial when the land thaws." He glanced at the contents of the cart, his heart clenching in his chest. "I hate to think of them lying in the dark and cold in the dugout near the church waiting for the spring. Marguerite hated the dark."

Pierre reached over and gripped his friend's shoulder in support. "*Oui*, I feel the same. But the women are with God now. Safe in his arms. The priest will make it so if we have any doubts."

"*Oui*, I suppose you are right." He crossed himself one more time.

Chapter Three

Guillaume trudged up the path toward his home, halting at the entry to organize his thoughts. The young ones still weren't aware their *maman* wasn't coming home. He scrubbed a hand over his face. What a thing to have to tell his nephews. Another thought coming hard on the heels of the first. How was he to care for the little ones? His job took him away from home regularly. The trips out to White Horse Plain to bring back buffalo robes and meat took much time, and depending on the weather, the length of his absences were unpredictable. Time enough to think of that later, he chided himself. Get to the matter at hand. Taking a steadying breath he pushed open the door.

Oncle Guillaume!" Alexandre threw himself at the tall man, wrapping his arms around his thighs.

Guillaume bent down and scooped the seven-year-old up in his arms. "Alexandre, have you been helping Fèlicitè care for your brother?' He settled the child on his hip and moved closer to the fire where Fèlicitè sat in Marguerite's rocker with Ètienne in her lap.

She smiled at him as he drew near and put a finger to her lips.

"The fever is broken. He is sleeping." She rose and placed him gently on the thick pallet by the hearth, safe behind the fire guard. "You look like you could use a hot drink and something to eat. Alex, would you sit with your brother for a moment, *sil vous plais*?"

Guillaume set the boy down and he obediently went to nestle by his brother's side. The two adults moved away to the far side of the small building.

"Did you find your sisters?" Fèlicitè kept her voice low. "Are they not with you? What has happened?" She peered up at him, trying to read his expression in the dim light.

He shook his head. "It is not good news, I'm afraid. I found them, yes. But they were attacked last night."

"Why are they not here then. We care for our own. Where did you leave them?" Fèlicitè demanded, slapping her hands on her hips.

"They are beyond our keeping now. They are in God's hands." The words came out harsher than he intended.

"*Non! Non!*" Fèlicitè hissed the words into her fisted hand jammed against her lips. "I wish they hadn't gone into the village at such an hour, but I understand why they did. Poor *bebes*." She glanced at the brothers drowsing by the fire. "Poor Alex is exhausted. He told me he sat up all night with Ètienne, wiping him down with cold water just like his *maman* told him. Thank God the fever broke when it did." She gave a strangled laugh. "The boy didn't need the *condamner* medicine at all, but how was anyone to know that at the time."

"I have to tell them." Guillaume turned his attention to his nephews. Alex was drooping beside Ètienne and even as they watched he lay down and curled up next to him.

"Let them sleep, *mon ami*. A few hours won't change anything, and they need the rest. As do you." She regarded him sternly.

"I have many things to take care of. The priest is wanting money for the care of the bodies, and I must speak with the Hudson Bay clerk this afternoon."

"You go do what you must. Have no fear, I will care for the boys. When they wake, I will take the children to my place." She waited a moment before adding. "I will leave it to you to tell them the sad news. It should come from family."

"*Merci*, Fèlicitè. You help is appreciated. Tell your papa I will speak with him later." With one last look at his sleeping nephews, Guillaume went out the door heading toward the Village of Winnipeg looking for answers.

* * *

Guillaume covered the distance from the clustered cabins of the Mètis community to the village in a haze of exhausted determination. His body moving as if of its own accord while his thoughts spun in a million directions. Someone must have seen something. The Hudson Bay store was his first stop. The clerks were terrible gossips, they quickly knew anything that went on in the village and surrounding area. The cold temperature helped chase the worst of the tiredness from his brain by the time he strode into the store. The heat in the place enveloped him, warming his nose and cheeks. There was frost on the buffalo hide on the backs of his gloves when he pulled them off and tucked them into his belt.

"Ah, Mousseau. What can we do for you this fine morning," the clerk, Alfred, greeted him, the Orkney tones of his voice still sounded odd to Guillaume's ears. Such a guttural sound when compared to the fluidity of the French tongue.

"Tobacco, to start. What have you heard about the bodies found by the river this morning?" He rested a hip against the counter.

Alfred was silent for a moment, indecision written across his features. "The bodies?"

"*Oui*, the bodies of two Mètis women. By the river this morning, beaten to death. My sisters." It wasn't how he'd planned to start the conversation, but he was too tired to engage in the dance of parry and thrust for

47

information which he would normally have used.

"I heard there was some kind of commotion this morning, important enough to get Ashmore out of his cozy house before breakfast. I had no idea it had anything to do with you, *Mousieur* Mousseau. My condolences."

"Oui, merci." He brushed the comments aside. "What have you heard? Men gather here and talk, have you heard any rumours about what happened by the river?"

Alfred shook his head. "Not this morning, but I've just come on duty. Simon!" He called into the storeroom behind the counter.

"Whatcha want?" Simon appeared in the doorway, holding the heavy woollen blanket that served as door aside. "Mousseau." He nodded at Guillaume when he noticed him at the counter.

"You hear any talk about what happened by the river this morning. Finding those bodies."

"Just that they was two Frenchies. The British don't seem to be takin' much interest from what I heard. Word is it was probably a liaison gone wrong." He waggled his eyebrows, his lips twisting in a lewd grin.

"Those women are my sisters," Guillaume's voice was low and hard. He was interested to note the pallor that washed over Simon's face. His gut said the man knew more than he was letting on.

"Umm, sorry. No offence meant. Just repeatin' what I heard, ya know." Simon disappeared into the storeroom, the curtain falling in place behind him.

"Anyone hear anything about those women found by the river?" He addressed the room at large. The majority of the men shook their heads, a few that he knew well came over to clap him on the shoulder and assure him they would let him know if they heard anything at all. The English half-breeds ignored him, which was typical, and the other men pretended interest in whatever was nearest them. It was nothing more than what Guillaume expected. But he had put the village on notice that he was not letting the incident die nor was he ever going to be content with the non-investigation by the British powers that be and Lord Ashmore in particular.

"Your tobacco." Alfred set the package on the counter.

Guillaume pulled a few coins from his belt pouch and dropped them on the counter. "*Merci.*" He left the store conscious of the eyes on his back as he shut the door. Where to next? Closing his eyes for a moment he searched his tired brain for the information the lord's sevant man had supplied. "The apothecary. Schultz's. *Oui,* that is where I must go." Stepping down off the wooden step he turned toward the pathway where Schultz's establishment was located.

"Mister." A ragged child, wrapped in so many rags as to be almost unrecognizable, hailed him seemingly appearing out of thin air. "Mister, I gotta talk ta you."

Guillaume halted. He didn't recognize the boy, for it was a boy he realized as he got closer. "What do you want? I have nothing for you?" The child was obviously a beggar, most likely an orphan or a runaway.

The thin shoulders straightened under the rags and the eyes narrowed. "Might be I have something you might be wantin' ta know."

"You are wasting my time. I have important things to care for." Guillaume began to move away.

"What if I was knowin' something about what went on last night by the river..." the lad let his words trail off.

Mousseau swung around so fast he almost knocked the boy off his feet. His hand fisted in the mess of material wrapped around the skinny body. "What do you know of my sisters?" he hissed, drawing the boy closer so the stink of his unwashed body clogged Guillaume's nose.

"You gonna try and beat it outta me?" The boy seemed resigned to his fate. "Won't do ya no good. I ain't tellin' without ya paying me some'at."

Guillaume relaxed his grip a bit, but not enough that the boy could pull loose. "What makes you think I am rich enough to pay you anything?"

The child snorted and gave him a most unchildlike glance. "Ya got a coat, ya got good boots and them buffalo gloves. I reckon you're one a' them Frenchie Half-breeds what travels between here and the Plains."

Guillaume glanced down at the rags wrapped around his captive's feet, bare frost-bitten toes peeking through in places. Fair enough, he thought and changed tack, the lad was obviously living rough, maybe he did see or hear something he thought was worth selling. "What is your name?"

The boy blinked twice and regarded him blankly. Guillaume gave him a gentle shake. "Your name?"

"What's it to you?" He stuck out his chin in a show of defiance.

"As you are asking payment of me, it seems we are to engage in an arrangement of sorts, and I like to know the name of the people I am dealing with. I am Guillaume Mousseau."

A calculating expression chased across the lad's face before he seemed to come to a decision and nodded. "I be Archie." He jabbed a bony thumb at his chest.

"Well then, Archie. Come with me." He swung the boy around, keeping an arm around his shoulder to prevent him from fleeing and started down the street.

"Where ya takin' me." Archie dug his feet in, resisting as best he could.

"I was thinking to feed you and see if my nephews have anything that might fit you."

He shrugged. "But if you have better things to do…"

Archie stopped resisting and plodded along by his side. "Nothin' better to do," he muttered.

"Where are your parents?" Guillaume said the first thing that came to mind. Anything to keep the boy distracted from escaping.

Archie snorted. "My pa is dead. Ma's back in the Orkneys." What he left unsaid was that he couldn't return home as he had no money and no way of getting any except by stealing.

"How long have you been in Rupert's Land?" They left the outskirts of the village, the cluster of the huts visible in the distance. Guillaume picked up his pace a bit. Anxious to get home and find out what Archie knew. Anything, no matter how small might prove to be important.

"Two years, near as I can reckon. I came over with Pa, and I bin here two winters."

"Ah, here we are." Guillaume drew him toward the cabin he had shared with his sisters. Ètienne and Alex would be with Fèlicitè so the place should be empty. He pushed Archie through the door first, securing it behind them. The lad bolted to the hearth warming himself at the smouldering fire. Guillaume stoked the blaze until it leaped and threw orange shadows along the walls. Archie sat cross-legged in its glare alternating between roasting his front and back. Guillaume couldn't help but notice how thin he was nor the pattern of dark bruises in various stages of healing. He shook his head. It was no concern of his, this Scottish child. But what if it was Alex...? He shoved the thought away. Archie had information, he hoped, that he needed. That was all, once he'd gotten it from him, Archie could go back to wherever it was he came from.

The pot of stew Marguerite had started the night before still hung near the fire. He swung it back into the heat and stirred it with the long wooden spoon. Archie's head came up like a questing stag, his gaze fixed on the bubbling pot. He rose to his knees and stuck a hand out. Guillaume batted it away.

"*Non*, you will burn yourself. In a moment I will get you a bowl." He took down a wooden bowl from the crude mantle shelf and ladled a good helping into it. Archie took the bowl and cradled it on his lap. Before he could dive in with his hands, Guillaume dropped a chunk of heavy bread beside him which Archie used to soak up the stew and stuff it in his mouth. When the bowl was licked clean and the boy was almost somnolent with food and heat, Guillaume decided it was time to find out just what it was the boy knew.

"Archie, are you ready to tell me what you think you know?" He sat cross legged beside the boy on the hearth stone.

"Don't think, I know!" he boasted turning toward his benefactor. "I was there, I saw it." His eyes widened with remembered horror.

Guillaume gripped his arm hard. "You saw who murdered them?"

Archie swallowed and looked pointedly at his arm. Guillaume loosened his grip. "Tell me everything. No matter how small."

"There's a bit of a lean to behind that house on the corner, you know. I sleep there some nights. It ain't much, but it cuts the wind, an' no one goes there."

Guillaume nodded, silently urging him to get to the point.

"Anyways, I was all set for the night, even managed to scrounge me another blanket. Then I heard someone sneaking around, even though it was windy and stormy, you know how snow squeaks when it's that cold. I near to shit myself. I was worried it was one of them men what likes young boys." He shot Guillaume a knowing, look. "There's more of 'em than you'd think."

Guillaume nodded. "Go on, what happened next."

"I hid as best I could, I was mortal glad I didn't have anything to start a fire with earlier. Whoever it was, they went right by the lean to, didn't even bother to look inside. I was some glad, I tell you."

"What did they do?" Guillaume shifted impatiently.

"Nothin' for a bit. I peeked out, curious like. I could see a figure lurking at the side of the house, like they was waiting for someone or something. It was the middle of the night and stormy. I couldn't for the life of me think what they was looking for. After a bit, I crawled back into the lean to, but I kept an eye on them just in case they decided to come my way. I must have dozed off 'cause the next thing I know there was women's voices, which was odd. I crept out on me hands and knees and the first thing I saw was the shadow by the house had moved. It was creeping toward the corner of the house closest the road. I couldn't see the women, but I heard them, they was deciding which way to go or something, but they were in a hurry. I just got a glimpse of two women when they passed the house. Next thing I see that guy that was lurking by the house for so long, stepped out from the building and hit the woman in front. The other woman called out and caught her as she fell. Then the man hit her too. It looked like she tried to fight, grabbed onto his coat as the two women fell, but it was dark and hard to see. And I sure as hell didn't want to let the man know I was there. I snuck back to the lean to as quick as I could and huddled under my blankets. I heard the person go by again, muttering under his breath." Archie shivered and pulled his rags closer in spite of the roaring fire. Gonna give me night horrors I reckon."

"What did he hit them with? Could you see? It is important." Guillaume prodded for more information.

"Something heavy. Maybe a knife, but it must have had a big handle. I never got a good look at it. Could'a bin a bat or a hunk of wood, maybe?"

"Clothing, what was the person wearing? Anything that stood out? Think Archie."

Archie wrinkled his forehead, closing his eyes. "Some kinda coat, long, maybe halfway down his legs. With buttons, I remember they kinda shone when he lit up a cigarette as he went by my hiding place. Boots, nice boots. I remember wishing I could cosh him and get them boots."

Guillaume ruffled the dirty hair. "Excellent so far. Now tell me, was it a big man, tall, thin. Fat?"

"He were pretty small. I remember being surprised when I saw that, thin and kinda slight. I mean the way he wacked those women I thought he'd be bigger." He winced at the pain that flashed across his benefactor's face, but wisely chose not to comment on it.

"You said he was muttering under his breath. Did you hear what he said?" Guillaume forced himself to concentrate on the words and ignore the image the words implanted in his mind.

"A bit, he were moving pretty quick once he got clear of the building. But then he stopped and started comin' back. I was scairt he'd seen me. But no, he went by again, out into the road and started a'dragging the women toward the river. I don't know how far he got 'cause I sure weren't goin' to go look. After a few minutes I heard more voices, sounded like men comin' from the saloon. Then the first man, the one what whacked the women, he comes sliding back behind the building, puffing like an ox."

"What did you hear him say?" It was hard to hold back his impatience.

"Somethin' about it servin' them right, who did they think they was, botherin' decent folks, another bit about bein' glad they was taken care of. Somethin' about somethin' he lost but couldn't risk goin' back to find it. Sounded like it was somethin' important to him..." Archie shrugged. "That's all."

Guillaume's fingers closed around the gold signet ring in his pouch. Something important, aye? Something that could place someone at the scene. He smiled.

"What now? Do I gotta go?" Archie tugged at his coat sleeve. "You said somewhat about gloves or a coat?" he asked a tentative, hopeful expression on his grimy face.

"*Oui*, I did, did I not." He unfolded his long frame in a fluid motion. "Let me see what I can find." He opened the wooden chest he'd made to house their extra belongings. Near the bottom he found a pair of gloves that would fit, he tossed them to the boy who scooped them up. There was an old pair of buckskin trousers which could be cut down and belted with one of the old frayed embroidered sashes. Provided the lad didn't mind looking like a French Half-breed. He pulled a heavy knitted sweater from a corner of the chest. One he'd bargained for that he'd hoped Alex would grow into. He tossed those over as well.

"Why you givin' me all this?" Archie held his booty to his chest, suspicion all over his face. "What else you be wantin' from me?"

"What?" Guillaume looked up, a pair of Marie-Anne's spare boots in his hands.

"What do you want besides what I can tell ya? Ain't nobody gives stuff away for nuthin'. I best be goin'." He struggled to his feet.

"Take these then and go." Guillaume tossed the boots in his direction.

Archie snatched the items up and edged toward the door.

"Go. *Veit*. I am not a lover of young boys. You asked for payment, and I have given it to you." He hurled the words at the huddled figure.

"You mean it. Ya ain't' expectin' me ta bend over for ya?"

"*Non!*" The word burst from him, laced with disgust. "I must go back to the village and to Fort Garry. I have much to attend to.

You may, if you wish, stay here. My nephews are with Fèlicitè, next door. I will let her know I have given you permission to stay by my fire. You are welcome to the food, so long as you don't steal from me. If you do, trust me, I will find you and it will not go well for you."

"Why?" Archie blinked at him in confusion. "I be less than nothing to you. Why are you being kind to me."

Guillaume sighed. "I would like to think that if my nephews were in such a state that someone would care for them. Also, I am grateful for the information you have given me. If you remember anything else, tell me immediately." He pulled his coat tighter around him and left the boy standing between the fire and the door. It took only a few moments to stick his head in at Fèlicitè's to check on his nephews and let her know of his visitor.

"When do you expect Baptiste, your papa?" he inquired, nodding hello to Fèlicitè's maman who tended something by the fire.

"Any time now. His party should only have been a few days behind yours. Did you see him out at the Plains?"

"*Oui*, we shared a fire for a few nights. The hunting is good. The Company store should be pleased."

Fèlicitè drew him away from the fire where the boys were playing. "They are asking for their *maman* and auntie. Are you ready to tell them? I think it wise before they hear it from someone gossiping."

"You are right, of course. But I dread it." He squared his shoulders and moved back toward the fire. "Boys, *mon ami*. Come, I have something to tell you." Alex came and plopped into his lap as soon as Guillaume settled himself by the fire, Ètienne leaned against his knee.

"When is *Maman* and auntie coming home. They were supposed to bring medicine for Ètienne from Papa." Alex looked up at his uncle.

"That is what I want to talk to you about. Your *maman* and auntie did go to get medicine for Ètienne. But something bad happened and they are not coming home. Do you understand?"

"But they will come later, *oui*?" Alex persisted. "*Maman* promised she would."

"Sometimes, things happen that we cannot foresee, Alex. This is one of those times. Your *maman* and auntie are with God now. They are with his angels watching over us. They are with Elizabeth now."

"But Elizabeth is dead. Father Tachè said Jesus called her home. He said I couldn't follow her until I was very old. *Maman* is not old," Alex insisted.

"You must be brave. For me, for Ètienne. For your *maman*. Do you understand?"

Tears welled in the child's eyes and Guillaume's heart twisted in his chest. Whoever did this, caused such pain would pay. Of that, he was sure. "I must go, I have things that needed attending. You will stay with Fèlicitè until I come for you, yes?"

Alex nodded while Ètienne sucked on the end of a blanket, seeming oblivious to his brother's distress. Guillaume set him by his brother and got to his feet. He stopped to give Fèlicitè a brief hug and thank her, before remembering to tell her about the guest in his own cabin. Her eyes widened in surprise, but she nodded when he explained the information the boy had supplied.

Chapter Four

Guillaume slipped out of Fèlicitè's cabin and turned toward the village. He halted at the sound of his name.

"Hey mister, wait, I remember something else." Archie's disheveled head stuck out Guillaume's door.

"What do you recall?" He moved to join the boy, both of them retreating to the warmth of the cabin.

"It were before I went to bed down in the lean to. I was on my way there, truth be told, when I saw two women being bothered by a couple of men by the saloon—"

"Which saloon? Monchamps or O'Lone's?" Guillaume interrupted him.

The boy screwed up his face in thought. "O'Lone's." He nodded his head.

"Then what happened?" Guillaume prompted him.

"Well, I just seen two men kinda crowding these women, they didn't seem to care for it at all, then one 'em showed the men some kinda paper and the beggars backed off. But I did hear them talkin' about maybe following the women and note be damned."

"Did you recognize the men. See them clearly?"

"Not real clear, but I know who they be. Came acrost on the same ship as me pa and me. Don't know their full name, just heard 'em called Simon and Mark."

"They're Orkney men?" Guillaume racked his brain searching for a recollection of any men by that name with a strong accent.

"Not Orkney. They came aboard in Liverpool, I think it was. I was pretty seasick and so glad for the ship to stop moving that I really didn't pay much attention to where we were."

"Ah, *bein sur*." The pieces fell together in his head. Both men by that name were employed at the Hudson Bay Company store. Time to go have a talk with them after he bearded Dr. Schulz in his den. *I wonder if Marguerite and Marie-Anne even made it as far as the apothecary.*

He patted Archie on the shoulder. "*Merci, mon ami*. That information is very helpful. Now think carefully. Could the person who hurt my sisters be one of these same men?"

"Archie hesitated. "I guess, maybe. The scrawnier one. Maybe, but I couldn't say for sure." He shrugged.

"No matter. I will look into this. You are welcome to stay here as long as you wish. Fèlicitè is aware and will not bother you. *Medna*, I am to the village to see what I can find." He paused by the door. "If you are ever in trouble in the village you can go to my friend Pierre. He works at the Nor-Wester. Tell him you are my friend, and he will do what he can for you."

"Why you being so nice to me, mister? I don't understand." Archie repeated his earlier doubts, although he didn't budge from his place by the fire.

"You remind me of my nephews and my younger brother who is no longer among the living. Is that sufficient to lay your fears to rest?"

Archie nodded and snuggled himself into Marguerite's rocking chair, swaddling himself in shawls.

Grinning, Guillaume shut the door behind him. The amusement fleeing as he turned his thoughts to the village. He made his way back to the Hudson Bay store, stopping just inside the door. Alfred was still behind the counter.

"Back so soon, Mousseau? What can I do for you?"

"Is Simon still in the storeroom?" Guillaume leaned against the counter, one elbow resting on the surface.

"I believe so, why? Do you need to speak with him about something?"

"If it is convenient." Guillaume could almost see the man's ears twitching at the prospect of gossip.

"I'll go see if he can be spared at the moment." Alfred disappeared into the back.

Forcing himself to remain leaning against the counter, Guillaume fingered the ring in his pouch. Who would have such a thing in their possession? It was small, but perhaps it would fit a small man's finger. It certainly didn't belong to either of his sisters, but could it have been dropped by someone totally unconnected to the murder? Possible, he supposed, not content to drop its appearance at the scene from his investigation.

"You wanted to see me?" Simon approached the counter. His step faltered when he realized who it was that wanted to talk to him.

"I do." Guillaume straightened up to his full height. "Were you at O'Lone's last night?"

"Maybe. Might 'a bin. What's it to you?" Colour rose in his face, contrasting with the weeks growth of whiskers bristling on his cheeks.

"There was a small matter of some men bothering a couple of women passing by. Would you know anything about that?" Guillaume watched the man's expression closely.

"Don't recall anything like that. That all you want?" He stepped back from the counter, preparing to return to the storeroom.

"I have spoken to some who recall you and your friend Mark speaking with these women. Do you deny this?"

Simon shook his head. "Whoever told you that was mistaken. Weren't me at all. I can't stand here all day talkin' to the likes of you. I got me work to do." He hurried into the storeroom, casting an apprehensive glance over his shoulder before the curtain fell into place.

Frustration roiled in Guillaume's gut. The *chien* was lying through his teeth, he would bet his last buffalo robe on it. He must find this Mark and see if he could be persuaded to sing a different tune.

"Did you get what you needed from Simon?" Alfred sidled down the counter from his vantage point where he'd listened to ever word between the men.

"I got what he was willing to give," he replied enigmatically, refusing to reveal anything further. "Do you know where Mark lives?"

"The clerk? He bunks with Simon at the company lodgings since neither of them have found a woman who will put up with them." Alfred shot a stream of tobacco juice into the brass spittoon and laughed.

Guillaume nodded and shoved his way to the door. He made his way toward Schultz's establishment. The man should be able to tell him if his sisters reached his store last night. *Merde!* Was it only this morning he'd found them? It seemed like days rather than hours had passed. He scrubbed a hand through his beard and hardened his resolve. Time enough to rest once he ran down all the information he could find. A few minutes walk brought him to his destination. He stepped into the store and waited while two well dressed English ladies chatted with Dr. Schultz. His attention was piqued when one of the ladies referred to the other as Charlotte. Was that not the name of Ashmore's English wife? Guillaume took closer note of the woman. Certainly pretty in that pale blonde way that so many Englishwomen seemed to appear. Pink bloomed on her cheeks, whether from the temperature in the store of from artifice he wasn't sure. Clearly expensive, and totally impractical clothing, he decided, peeked out from under a thick fur lined cloak. This hot house flower was what the man preferred to Marguerite? He shook his head in wonderment. The foolishness of the Englishmen never failed to astound him. His suspicions as to her identity were confirmed when Schultz finished compounding whatever it was he'd been working on and folded it up into a neat package.

"Here you are, Lady Ashmore. I do hope your servant is feeling better soon." Schultz pushed the package toward her. He paused. "Will your husband be in to take care of the medicine he asked me to supply last night?"

Charlotte Ashmore looked down her aquiline nose at him and sniffed. "I'm sure I don't know what you are referring to. You will have to take that up with Lord Ashmore himself." She turned on her heel and caught sight of Guillaume standing a polite distance from her and her companion. She reared back as though she had come across a snake unexpectedly. "Really, Doctor Schultz. You should be more careful of your clientele." The two women swept by him in a swirl of heady perfume and swish of cloth. The door swung shut on the other woman's words, though the scent of lavender lingered behind them.

"Really, Charlotte. It is most inconvenient your man servant is ill. However, did he catch a chill?"

Charlotte's reply was muffled by the closing door. Interesting, Guillaume thought, how would that man catch cold when he never seemed to venture outside the confines of the house. Interesting, indeed. Another piece of his puzzle perhaps? Perhaps not.

He moved from the doorway and approached the counter, aware of the man's eyes on him. Distrusting and judgmental.

"Doctor Schultz, my sisters came to the village last night to get some medicine for my nephew. Do you recall two women coming in with a note from Lord Ashmore?" Guillaume approached the counter.

"I do recall as a matter of fact, and dashed inconvenient it was too. I was closed when they came banging on the door. What of it?"

"What time was it when they left here?"

"I don't remember, man. It was late. If it hadn't been for Ashmore's note, I would have sent them packing, told them to come back in the morning at a reasonable hour." Schulz crossed his arms over his chest and glared over his half-moon spectacles.

"If you could be more specific about the time," Guillaume persisted.

"I told you I don't recall, and I don't. What does it matter? I gave them the medicine they came for and I've yet to be paid for it."

Guillaume ignored the less than subtle request for payment. Let Ashmore deal with it. "Those women never made it home, Doctor Schultz. You are possibly the last person to see them alive."

"What are you implying?" The doctor's mouth thinned, a red flush creeping up his throat.

"I'm not implying anything. It would be a great help if you could give me even an idea of the time."

"Said I don't recall." He snapped his mouth shut and turned to shuffle things around in his medicine cabinet. When Guillaume remained by the counter, he glared over his shoulder at him. "Why are you still here? I've told you all I can. Now get out."

Guillaume considered other actions but instead left the shop without a word. He strode down the lane, heedless of where he was going, mind whirling with thought in the attempt to put the information he'd managed to gather into a rational sequence. He changed direction in mid-stride, perhaps it was time to pay the Hudson Bay Company offices a visit. Simon had been less than forthcoming with information, but perhaps his fellow employee, Mark, would be able to confirm or deny Archie's story about the two men accosting the women. He paused to consider for a moment. If they came from Ashmore's house, their path would have taken past both Monchamps and O'Lone's saloons on the way to Schultz's.

Now, he knew they had actually made it as far as Schultz's, he would have to travel to Fort Garry and ask the Father to allow him to examine the bodies. *Merde!* Why didn't he think to search their pockets before leaving them in the church's keeping? The Father was a good man, in all likely hood nothing on his sisters' bodies would be disturbed. Although, he supposed the Grey Nuns might have already stripped and cleaned the bodies. His stomach curled and his reason rebelled when he found himself thinking of Marguerite and Marie-Anne as bodies. He meant no disrespect, but somehow it was easier to distance himself from the grief if one part of his mind thought of them in that way. One way or another, he resolved to keep searching until he found out who murdered them. The Hudson Bay men who oversaw the justice system and courts were already aware, but as far as Guillaume knew they were doing nothing about the incident. Typical, he thought.

Was the British lord trying to hush the whole thing up? He'd made no secret of his wish for Marguerite and the children to vanish back into the French Half-breed community, and as far as he was concerned, cease to exist. Perhaps he was behind this horrible event. That would make Guillaume's job harder. How was he to go up against the English when they, and their compatriots, ran the village.

His arrival at the Hudson Bay Company offices interrupted his musings. Shaking his head to clear it, he entered the building and asked to speak with the Chief Factor. The clerk at the front desk shuffled some papers and finally acknowledged Guillaume's presence.

"I'm sure he's too busy to see you at the moment," he dismissed Guillaume's request out of hand.

Guillaume propped both elbows on the high counter and leaned toward the man. "Perhaps if you inform him that I have some questions regarding two of his employees and the death of two women last night, he will find he has the time." Guillaume failed to disguise the menace in his tones.

The clerk blinked and backed up a step. His gaze travelled over the breadth of Guillaume's shoulders and the grim expression on his face. "I will see if Mister Adams is available." He hurried away, leaving Guillaume to his own devices. A couple of clerks working at nearby desks looked up at the disturbance but quickly lost interest. Leaning with his back against the counter, Guillaume surveyed the area of the offices he could see. What was taking the man so long? He'd almost decided it was time to take matters into his own hands and go in search of the man in question himself when the clerk came scurrying back.

"He'll see you now, if you'll come this way." Keeping a safe distance between himself and Guillaume, the clerk escorted him through a door and down a hallway, stopping at a closed door and knocking.

"Come." The voice was imperious and impatient.

The clerk pushed the door open and stepped away to let Guillaume enter, closing the door after he went past.

"What is it that is so imperative that you feel you must disturb me at my work?" The HBC Chief Factor steepled his fingers and looked down his nose at the tall man dressed in buckskin with the bright red embroidered sash around his waist standing before him. He did not offer the man a seat.

Guillaume ignored the snub, returning the man's stare. "I'm sure by now you've heard about the murders that occurred by the river last night or early this morning."

"What of it? Murders, you say? I heard it was two unfortunates who were perhaps plying their trade and the encounter went wrong. What has that to do with the Hudson Bay Company?"

"Those women were my sisters," he ground the words out. "They were not plying any *trade*, but instead were in the village to get medicine for a sick child. I assure you it was murder."

"Again, I ask, what has this to do with the Hudson Bay Company? If you have a complaint, you can bring it up at the Quarterly Court Session." His tone implying he had far more important things demanding his attention.

"I have heard that my sisters were accosted near O'Lone's by two men who are employed by your company. I would very much like to speak with them. In fact, I have already spoken with Simon at the store earlier today. I wish to speak with Mark, who is the other man identified as bothering the women."

"I'm sure my employees had nothing to do with any of this. You are wasting your time and mine." He flipped open a ledger on his desk in a clear dismissal.

Guillaume planted both large hands on the desk and leaned toward the man. "Perhaps if I inform you that one of women was Marguerite Mousseau who looked after Lord Ashmore before he brought his English wife to the village you might find the time."

"The man looked up from the pages. "If the lord wishes my co-operation in this affair, I am sure he will contact me himself. Please remove yourself from my office."

Frustrated, but realizing he was getting nowhere, Guillaume slammed his palms down on the desk before striding out, leaving the door swinging behind him. "Stinking English *saloud*!" he swore under his breath. He would have to find this Mark himself. It shouldn't be too hard. He'd just watch the company store until the clerk came on duty. Or he could hang around the saloons until he showed up. Every man showed up at the drinking establishments at some point when they got their pay packets and it was almost month end.

In the meantime, he would drop by the Nor'Wester office and see how Pierre was managing. He and Marie-Anne had enjoyed a close relationship, and Guillaume was fairly sure Pierre intended to ask Marie-Anne to marry him. He couldn't imagine how his friend must be feeling. Guillaume was having a hard enough time dealing with losing his sisters. He wasn't sure what to say to Pierre, but he needed to find out if he had heard anything more, or different, about the murders than Guillaume managed to find out. It would be good to tell him what he learned from Archie, perhaps talking it out would help him get it clear in his mind. Maybe see a pattern he was missing or something important he'd overlooked.

He jumped over an icy puddle at the foot of the steps, the gold ring and the silver button in his pouch chimed as he landed. His fingers touched them through the pouch at his belt. Before he saw Pierre perhaps he should visit Mister Thompson. His little business was quite a growing concern catering to the ruling class of the settlement. The man did a fair trade in tailoring and repairing the fine clothes of the English and Scots of the community. Thompson might recognize the button and be able to tell Guillaume who it might belong to. He deviated from his current course and headed toward Thompson's which was located on one of the narrow laneways running at right angles from King Street toward the river.

Chapter Five

"Ah, Mister Mousseau, what brings you in my door this afternoon?"

Thompson was a friendly sort, never exhibiting any prejudice toward either the native population or the half-breed communities, either French or English. Guillaume actually liked the little man, although he'd never done business with him.

"A question only, *Monsieur* Thompson. I have found this button in the street, and I wondered if you could tell me who it might belong to. Guillaume pulled the object in question from his pouch and handed it to Thompson.

The little man turned it over in his hand, then moved closer to the window to examine it in the pale sunlight filtering through the thin waxed rawhide that did little to keep out the cold but did block the worst of the wind. He scratched his head and peered at the raised markings on the front of the button. Guillaume tamped down his impatience. The chances of Thompson actually being able to identify the possible owner were slim, but any information would be a help. At least that was his fervent hope.

Thompson turned from the window and handed the button back to Guillaume who tucked it back in his pouch.

"A moment," he said. There was a crockery pot on the pot belly stove that warmed the space. Thompson picked it up and filled two clay mugs, offering one to Guillaume. "Only tea, I'm afraid. I don't indulge in the hard stuff."

"*Merci.*" Guillaume accepted the mug of tea, appreciating the gesture of hospitality that was usually so lacking from a member of the Scots and English population of Winnipeg.

Thompson indicated two chairs by the stove. "Come, sit for a moment."

Once the two men were settled and Thompson had poked up the fire, the little man leaned back and regarded his companion.

"I imagine this has something to do with the death of your sisters?" he smiled at Guillaume's start of surprise. "News travels fast, my friend. I wish I could be of more assistance. But what I can tell you is that the button is indeed silver, not gilt or nickel. Therefore it either came from a piece of expensive clothing, most likely British or Scottish, or from the livery of a high placed servant. Although it might have been won by someone gambling with one of them."

"That is more information than I had before, *merci.*" He gave a brief bow of his head. "There is some kind of raised pattern on the face of it, do you recognize it at all?"

Thompson shook his head. "The embossing is quite worn, so the button is not new, I would guess it came from England at some point. The back is quite broken which suggests it was torn from the original garment rather than falling off from wear and tear. I don't recognize the pattern at all, which leads me to venture a guess that it was originally a coat of arms or some such." He paused and nodded to the clothing hanging at the back of his establishment, neatly labeled, and waiting for pickup. "I do a great deal of repairs for the English and so am familiar with most of the crests. However, I do not claim to recognize them all."

Guillaume drained the last of his tea and got to his feet, setting the mug on the stove beside the pot. "You have been most helpful."

Thompson got to his feet as well. "I'm happy I could assist you. I knew your sisters quite well, I'm not sure if you are aware of that fact. They often took on some embroidery for me, for ladies' handkerchiefs and other fripperies which the ladies require. Such a shame and such a waste..." He shook his head. "I wish you every success in finding who did this."

Guillaume nodded; his throat too full to allow speech. Such kindness in an unexpected place took him off guard and allowed his grief to rise to the surface of his thoughts. He strode from the building, surprised to find the last light of the sun throwing blood red shadows across the village. The vista matched his sombre mood.

* * *

Pierre was up to his elbows in lead type face and printers' ink when Guillaume arrived at the Nor'Wester's office. He waited until Pierre was done setting the last of the type in place before tightening the mast and setting the press in motion, spending the time to muse about the atmosphere of unrest being stirred up by the confrontations between Riel and Canadian representatives.

Mister Coldwell was absent, most likely off seeing what information he could gather for the next edition. There was a wave of resentment sweeping the community over the upstart Canadian government pushing their way in and running roughshod over the inhabitants already established along the river. The original settlers had set out the plots in the old French system of long thin lots with each one having river frontage and so having access to water and easy transportation via the river. Now the upstart representative of the new Canada Party was running their survey lines all over the established properties, setting out larger square portions which would severely limit access to the river. In addition, they were displacing the French and English Half-breed communities and allotting the land to the new immigrants coming from the east and Upper Canada. The Canadian Prime Minister Sir John A Macdonald seemed to have no idea that Rupert's Land and the area around the village of Winnipeg and Fort Garry was already settled. Trouble was coming, Guillaume was certain of it. His sympathies lay with Louis Riel and his talk of resistance.

Pierre emerged from the back, wiping his ink-stained hands on an equally ink stained rag. "I'm almost done for the day, just one sheet left to print. I can get it done early tomorrow morning. Do you have time for a drink or do you have to get home. Who is taking care of the little ones?"

"Fèlicitè, is watching Alex and Ètienne. I have much to tell you though, it has been a long and busy day. Also, I must return to Fort Garry tomorrow and ask the Father to let me examine Marguerite and Marie-Anne, or at least their clothing."

"Why does that matter?" Pierre frowned. "Were they carrying something valuable? Is that why you think they were attacked?"

"*Non, non.* I spoke with Schultz, and he confirmed they did make it that far and they had gotten the medicine for Ètienne from him because they gave him a note from the Englishman. In which case, they must have gone to Ashmore's first, then to the apothecary. I have found out they were bothered by two men as they passed

O'Lone's, but obviously they did mange to get as far as Schutlz's."

"Any idea why they were by the river? Do you think someone was chasing them after they left the apothecary?"

"Gentlemen," Mister Coldwell addressed them as he breezed through the door. "I hope you have the next edition well in hand, Pierre." He nodded toward the absence of clanking coming from the back room where the human driven press sat silent. "I'll be here for a bit longer if you would like to go now. I'm sure you have some things that need taking care of after the events of the day." His gaze shifted from his employee to Guillaume and back.

"It is just the last sheet that needs printing, I can fold and distribute it first thing in the morning." Pierre shrugged out of his canvas apron and into his jacket. Outside, darkness pressed against the window. This late in the fall, the days were short and the nights interminably long.

"Run along, I'll see you in the morning, bright and early." Coldwell laughed. "Well, not bright but certainly early." He sat at his cluttered desk and pulled a sheaf of notes out of his jacket. "I've lots of news from Begg that I need to get on paper and send off to the Toronto Globe. Riel is certainly kicking up a storm. The readers will eat it up."

The two men left him still muttering as he poured over the notes and set about inscribing them neatly onto parchment. By unspoken accord they headed toward O'Lone's establishment. A group of Englishmen passed them, the woollen coats in sharp contrast to the buckskins and mish mash of other costumes the majority of men wore. After dark, women were conspicuous by their absence on the streets. Guillaume glanced at the men as they passed, the man nearest him at the back was missing a button on his coat making it hang differently than his fellow. Guillaume imprinted the features in his mind, he would know the man when he came across him again. He gripped the button in his pouch. Would it be a match for the buttons on the man's coat? According to Thompson most likely not, but Guillaume wasn't ready to rule anything out just yet.

"You alright?" Pierre bumped his shoulder. "You know those men?"

"Non, but one of them was missing a button on his coat. A silver button."

Pierre swung around to glare after the group and took a step in that direction.

"We can't confront them, they'd like nothing better than to throw us in jail, you know that. We will find out who that man is, and if he is responsible, he will pay. I promise you."

"I know you are right, but I have this anger in me that just wants to strike out at anyone who might have had a hand in hurting Marie-Anne."

"You are not alone in that feeling, *mon ami*. But we must go carefully, we must be wary of the English and the long arm of the Hudson Bay Company. I visited the headquarters today and Mister Adams was less than helpful. As much as told me that his employees were blameless, and I would do well to take my questions elsewhere. And there is always the religious interference, the Episcopalians are already starting rumours about the Roman Catholic women who were murdered, saying they shouldn't have been out alone at that time of night without nefarious reasons. They completely ignore the fact they were collecting medicine for a sick child." Guillaume spat in the dirt.

The noise and light spilled out of the saloon onto the road just ahead of them. "Come, *mon frere*, a few drinks will help settle our spirits." Pierre pulled him into the saloon.

Guillaume shoved his way to the bar and ordered two pints. He laid the coins on the bar where the greasy bar keep swept them into the pocket of his apron. Pierre touched his mug to Guillaume's and drank deeply. Guillaume brought his to his mouth but didn't drink. Snatches of conversation whirled around him, and he sifted through it, looking for anything that might aid his search. Most men drank in the same place every night, so chances were good that most of the men had also been drinking here last evening. Over the rim of his mug he scanned the florid faces jamming the saloon, searching for Simon and his friend Mark.

Maybe too early yet, he thought. Well, he had all night.

Merde! The sudden recollection of the Orkney orphan presumably still inhabiting his cabin brought him up short. How had that totally slipped his mind? He shrugged, nothing to be done about it now, and so long as the boy didn't set the place on fire or rob him blind, he was safe there. If the murderer got wind of the fact someone actually saw them attack the women, and figured out who it was, the boy's life was forfeit. No one would care if a ragged homeless orphan disappeared. The thought sent a chill down Guillaume's spine. Not that he was fond of the boy, but he had provided some very interesting information.

Pierre set his empty mug on the bar and indicated a refill. Guillaume dumped most of his on the floor without anyone being the wiser and let the bar keep fill his as well. This was a night he needed to keep his wits about him. The mass of men parted when newcomers entered, closing around them as they moved further into the room. Guillaume took note of each new group, but so far no one of interest had showed up. Perhaps this was just a big waste of time. His body ached with exhaustion, during the long trek back from the Plains laden with the robes and meat all he had thought about was sleeping in his own space and the welcoming scent of his sisters' cooking as well as regaling his nephews with tales of his adventures. Only yesterday, but it seemed as if years had passed. For the first time in his thirty-five years he felt old.

Voices rose above the general din of the saloon, a jolt of recognition shot through him. *Simon*. He'd know that voice anywhere now. In spite of the tension in his shoulders, he turned as casually as he could manage and leaned back against the bar. Pierre glanced sideways in surprise; ale held halfway to his mouth. Guillaume scanned the milling crowd searching for Simon. Luck was with him, the man shoved his way to the bar, ending up on the other side of Pierre. Guillaume elbowed his friend and passed him some coins under the edge of the bar, poking his chin in the Hudson Bay man's direction. Taking the hint, Pierre jostled the man.

"Watch it, Frenchie," Simon growled.

"*Pardon ai moi*, let me buy you a pint," Pierre responded. "Bar keep! A pint for this man."

"If yer buying, ye might as well buy me friend a pint as well." He sneered. "Hey, Mark. Over here, mate."

Guillaume couldn't believe his luck, the very man he was looking for dropped into his lap.

Pierre paid for the ale and started to step away. Guillaume made a move to stop him, but Simon beat him to it. The man threw an arm around Pierre's shoulder, holding him in place. Stick around, my friend. The night is young."

Guillaume turned his back on the three men, leaning a hip against the bar and pretending interest in what was happening at one of the tables where voices were raised. In reality, his attention was focussed on the conversation of Pierre and the other two men. Most of it was enough to put a man to sleep. A lot of belly aching about the people they worked with and for. Complaining about the conditions they were forced to live in, nothing like what they were promised by the Company recruiters in the old country. Guillaume almost tuned them out, until Pierre seized an opportune break in the conversation to supply some more ale and introduce the subject that Guillaume was interested in.

"I heard there was a bit of ruckus last night. A couple of women out on the street after dark were roughed up by some men outside this saloon. Any truth in it? Were you two here then to see any of it?"

"Nah," Simon spoke first.

"Yeah, we were, Simon." Mark broke in, leaning toward Pierre with a drunken leer. "Two of 'em. Not the usual type of skirt you see on the streets at night. The one of 'em was pretty toothsome, I have to say."

"You saw the ruckus then. How many men were there? Sounded like a group of them…"

Mark snorted ale out his nose as he laughed. "Wasn't that way at all. It was just the two of us, right Simon? Simon? Where did he go?"

When Mark started to brag about the incident, Simon had the presence of mind to drift away from the bar and lose himself in the crowd. Guillaume noted the movement but ignored it. He'd already spoken to the man and gotten nowhere. Perhaps his friend could be persuaded to be more forthcoming.

"What happened? Were the women friendly like?" Pierre prompted.

"Not at all. The one tried to knee me in me parts before we let 'em go." Mark scowled and took a long drink of ale.

"Why'd you let them go?" Pierre raised his eyebrows. "Seems like you could have gotten what you wanted from them..."

"Would've done, 'ceptin' they had a note from the English lord, sealed and all. Saying they was supposed to get some medicine and bring it back to the lord's house. We didn't want no trouble with that."

Guillaume moved around Pierre and gripped the man by the arm.

"Hey, watcha doing?" he protested.

Guillaume tightened his grip and Mark's face paled. He allowed himself to be frogmarched out the door and into the alley by the saloon. Pierre followed them out.

Gripping the man by the collar, Guillaume lifted him almost off his feet and pinned him against the wall. "You will tell me everything about what happened. Did you follow those women after you let them go? Wait until after they'd gone to Schultz's?" He shook the man and banged his head against the wood.

"What's it to you, Frenchie?" Mark spat in his face.

Guillaume head butted him before leaning back to avoid the spray of blood from the man's broken nose. "Those women were my sisters, *chein*. And now they are dead, left on the riverbank like offal. I will ask you again. Did you and your friend follow them after you let them go?"

Mark shook his head, blood and snot dripping in strings down his shirt. "No, we went back inside and drank some more. Them two were more trouble than they were worth."

Guillaume reached down and grabbed the man's right hand, fingers searching for an indentation where a ring might have sat that was now lost. The right hand held only callus, so he moved to the left. Again, nothing and the fingers were too thick at any rate. Frustration fueled his temper. "Think twice before bothering any other woman of my community," he growled. Pulling back his arm he landed a fist first in the man's belly and then when he doubled over, Guillaume sent Mark's head rocketing backward with a punch that made his knuckles sting and vibrated up his arm into his shoulder. He stepped back and let the

Company man slide down the wall where he toppled over on his side.

"Let's go," Pierre called from the end of the building. "Someone's coming."

Guillaume took a moment to check the fallen man's clothing. Nothing but the usual bone and wood buttons. Another dead end, *sacrè bleu*."

"Guillaume," Pierre hissed from the shadows. The two men faded into the darkness at the back of the building and worked their way along the building , emerging onto the street a distance away from the clot of men peering into the alley by the saloon.

They sauntered along the road, skirting the group of onlookers who were peering into the alley by the saloon. After hesitating long enough to avoid suspicion, they carried on toward the Nor'Wester offices where Pierre sometimes slept. The windows were dark so Coldwell must have left already. Guillaume refused his friend's offer to come in and warm up before the long walk back to his home. It was time he was getting back, and Jesu only knew what the boy had been up to in his absence.

The walk helped clear his head. He made a mental list of who might have wanted to harm Marguerite and Marie-Anne. Lord Ashmore was the first person who came to mind, but he most likely wouldn't dirty his hands, he'd have someone do it for him. The clerk Mark was most likely not the murderer, but what of Simon? Something about the way he looked when Guillaume questioned him seemed wrong, as if he was hiding something, or afraid. That one would bear thinking about, but carefully, the Hudson Bay Company decided all the disputes in the area, so they would be very reluctant to charge one of their own with such a crime. Not to mention the HBC Chief Factor had already told Guillaume to mind his own business. *Who else?* The boy said he saw a small man, who smoked. That wasn't much help, most men smoked, although the height and stature was a bit unusual. The ring and silver button bothered him. Perhaps the ring had nothing to do with anything, it was just chance he'd found it where he did, but the silver button...ah now there was something to be considered. It must have come from the murderer. Marguerite would have no reason to be in possession of a silver button. Even if she had taken on a job for one of the English ladies, the button would have been at home, not clutched in her hand in the dead of the night. An Englishman then. That prospect seemed far more likely than one of the few servants employed by the English and Scots who brought a few trusted employees with them from Upper Canada.

He lifted his head at the sound of his name. While he'd been turning things over in his mind, he hadn't realized he'd reached the collection of cabins where he lived.

"Gaston, *boujour.*" He greeted the man with a slap on the back and brief one-armed hug.

"Guillaume, I'm sorry about your sisters. I just got back from the Plains and heard the news. Do you have any idea who would do such a thing? The women are worried, no one is going anywhere alone."

"*Non*, not yet. But I will keep looking until I find them. Can you spare your oldest daughter to help care for Marguerite's children? Fèlicitè has taken them for now. If Brigette could watch them if Fèlicitè is needed at home, it would be a great help."

"Tell her to bring them to us if she needs to. It will be just as easy to take care of them with my family than having Brigette alone at your house."

Guillaume laughed. "Yes, that arrangement will suit very well. *Merc*i. I will let Fèlicitè know." He continued toward his home, the thought of Fèlicitè foremost in his mind. She was a quiet girl, well he supposed, she was a woman now having reached the age of nineteen, what some would consider far past time for her to be married with babies in tow. Marguerite and Marie-Anne were always after him to marry, but the idea had left him cold until now. He needed someone to look after the boys, not to mention the thought of someone to warm his bed during the long winter nights did have a certain appeal. *Phah!* Guillaume shook his head, time enough to worry about that later.

He pushed open his door, startling Archie who leaped to his feet, eyes darting in every which way seeking an escape route.

"*Mon ami*, it is only me. Calm yourself." Guillaume moved to add more fuel to the fire. The boy had let it die down to glowing embers and the cold was creeping in. Soon the flames were leaping, throwing wavering shadows on the crude wooden walls. The sight brought back memories of the tales he used to make up to entertain his younger sisters. He hadn't thought of that in years. Must be the presence of the boy, now curled up in the rocker with his blanket of shawls again.

"Ye got some'at to eat, mister?" Archie poked his head out of his nest, eyes wide in his thin face.

Hiding a smile, Guillaume moved toward the door.

"You ain't gonna throw me out, are you?" The youth sounded panicked.

"Got some venison hanging in the lean to." Guillaume slipped out the door and returned moments later with two strips of meat which he lay on the small table. Using Marie-Anne's butcher knife he lost no time in chopping the frozen meat into pieces and adding them to the ever-present stew pot over the fire. He sat in the willow chair opposite Archie and regarded the boy. "Quel âge as-tu? Pardon, I mean to say, how old are you?"

Archie drew himself up, shrugging the shawls off his shoulders. "I'm twelve. I ain't no boy no more. I can do the work of a man and earn my keep, if only someone would hire me."

Twelve? Guillaume would have guessed his guest was no more than nine or ten. "*Bein*! Then I will hire you." He held up a hand to stay the questions he saw forming in Archie's eyes. "I need you to go back to the village and do whatever it is you usually do there. Lurk around, listen to gossip, steal food?" He raised an eyebrow.

Archie flushed but nodded.

"I will speak with Pierre and see if Mister Coldwell would be willing to have a few words with Hugh O'Lone about letting you sweep up the saloon and perhaps pick up empty mugs. But what I wish from you is that you pay attention to everything that goes on. Who is drinking with who, you will be ignored as too ignorant and beneath their notice by the Hudson Bay men who drink there and any of the English, so they will speak freely. Your job is to be as invisible as possible and listen to every word."

"You want me to listen for anybody talking about the murder, 'specially if they was to sound like maybe they knew some'at." Archie nodded his head, considering the idea. "Reckon I can do that. The pennies I gets from O'Lone, I need to turn 'em over to you?"

Guillaume nodded in approval; the boy was sharper than he thought. "No, of course not. In addition, you can sleep here and are welcome to whatever food I have. Just be sure no one in the village is aware of where you sleep. We have a deal, *oui*?" He rose and offered his hand to the bundle of shawls.

Archie blinked at the offered hand. "Suits me to the ground." He shook himself free of the shawls and got to his feet before gripping Guillaume's hand.

"*Bein.* You can sleep there." He pointed to a rolled-up pallet, indicating Archie could roll it out by the fire and sleep quite comfortably. When he checked the level of water in the small barrel kept beside the hearth, he was pleasantly surprised to find that Archie must have taken the initiative to haul buckets in and fill the barrel as well as stocking the supply of wood in the wood box by the door. Better and better. As an afterthought, he turned back to the fire where Archie was now stretched out on the pallet, dark eyes following his benefactor's every move. "You don't have a liking for drink, do you?" it was not uncommon for even boys younger than Archie to indulge in spirits or ale, either provided by their papas or stolen from the caches of others in the settlement or more dangerously from the supplies held by the saloons.

"Not me," Archie declared. "Ma says drinking is the devil's work. Even Pa didn't drink much back home…" His words trailed off, giving the impression all that changed once he and his pa arrived in Rupert's Land.

"*Bien*. I need you to keep your wits about you. You can wander back into the village tomorrow. Get some sleep tonight." Guillaume waited until Archie's breathing told him he was asleep before slipping out the door to join a group of men who were in support of the French Half-breeds idea of a provisional government to negotiate with the Canadian government who seemed to think they could just show up and take over without taking into account the fact that there was already a thriving established settlement under the jurisdiction of the Hudson Bay Company. There were plans underway to blockade the road from Pembina and keep McDougall from reaching Fort Garry. The plan was for him to set up house in Silver Heights, the house in St James that had been made ready for him by the English that supported the annexation of Rupert's Land by Canada.

Guillaume wanted no part of any violence, but he was appalled at the stupidity of the Canadian government in their total disregard for those already living in the area. Howe had been to the area and seemed a reasonable man, surely his report of the current situation would be taken into account. Many of the English, in particular some of the newspapers, were spreading scandalous rumours about the way the Hudson Bay Company conducted themselves. All of it lies, as far as Guillaume was concerned. How could those who lived far away in a totally different society claim to know how things in the settlement were.

From what he had seen, the Canadian government intended to let the current population have no voice in the new way of doing things and no consideration was being given to those with established farms. The surveyor seemed a likable reasonable man, but he had his orders and those were to chop up the land in a way the new government, which hadn't even taken control yet, demanded.

The French Half-breeds were leading the opposition, under John Bruce, the president, and secretary, Louis Riel of the National Committee of the Mètis of Red River. Guillaume's views were in accordance with the majority of the community. He wished the English Half-breeds would take a more active role, as they were being affected as well, but they seemed to be content to wait and see if the incoming government would keep its promises to include them in the negotiations. Guillaume doubted those promises would be kept.

It was well past midnight when he left the gathering and made his way home. Nothing was resolved, other than an agreement that McDougall must leave Pembina and retreat back onto the America side. His wife and servants had reportedly already been sent back to St Cloud to wait out the winter. But none of this unrest was bringing him any closer to exposing his sisters' murderer. He scrubbed a hand over his face and pushed open the door, stepping into the welcome warmth.

"Only me," he assured Archie who had popped up out of his blankets when the door opened. Blinking, he subsided back into his blankets and rolled toward the fire.

Guillaume hung his jacket on a peg by the door and dropped the bar into place before seeking his own bed. He supposed he could use the box bed his sisters used to share but decided he would leave it for now. Instead, he unrolled the blankets on his pallet by the fire and settled himself for the night.

Chapter six

Roused by the banging on the door, Guillaume surfaced from the nest of blankets and shook his head to clear away the sleep fogging his brain. "*Un moment*," he called, untangling his long legs, and stepping over Archie to reach the door. "*Qu'est ce?*"

"*C'est moi, Francois*," came the reply.

"*Ah, oui.*" Guillaume removed the bar and opened the door. "*Entré tu.*" He stepped back to allow the man in. Scratching his head, he moved to stir up the fire, add a log and shove the iron kettle into the coals.

Archie scrambled out of his bed roll and used the pot in the corner to relieve himself.

"I was sorry to hear about your sisters, *mon ami.*" Francois clapped his friend on the shoulder.

"*Merci*, I am determined to find the *saloud* who did this."

"Perhaps you will hear something of interest on the way to the plains. It is time to make the trip again."

"I suppose it is, I have lost track of the time with everything that has happened."

"Are you bringing the *jeune garçon* with us this time?" Francois eyed the English boy with some trepidation. "Where did you find this one?"

Guillaume considered for moment, before turning to Archie. "How do you feel about coming with us to the White Horse Plains? It is a fair journey, and the work is hard."

Archie drew himself up to his full five-foot-four height and squared his shoulders. "I'm your man," he declared. "I ain't afeared of hard work, and I owe ya for the grub and the bed."

"Good man! *Beau!*" He turned to Francois. "How many ox carts are we taking this time?"

"Ten, I believe. I wish it were spring instead of early winter. I'm tired of the cold and snow already."

"As am I," Guillaume agreed. "When do we leave?" He added some ground chicory to the boiling water and waited for it to boil again. He and Francois sat at the table while Archie scurried about packing what he thought would be needed on the trip. Guillaume watched him with satisfaction, the boy had a good grasp of the necessities. When the chicory mixture had gotten strong enough, he poured three clay mugs and gestured for Archie to join them at the table.

"You will come, *oui*, but you will stay out of the way and not cause any trouble. You will also keep you ears open for anything that I might find interesting," Guillaume cautioned the boy.

Archie nodded and sucked on his mug of chicory coffee. "How far is it to this plain place?"

"Somewhere in the range of twenty-five miles. It will not be an easy journey with the ox carts over the frozen track, and in some places, it is most likely starting to get icy after the recent storm," Francois told him.

"That's a fair long way." Archie wrinkled his forehead. "Where do we sleep?"

Guillaume laughed and ruffled the boy's hair. "Wherever you can. Whenever you can."

Francois finished his mug and set it on the table. "We leave as soon as the sun comes up." He slapped Guillaume on the shoulder. "I will see you soon." He took his leave, closing the door behind him.

Archie cleared the table and started rooting in the supplies, packing jerky and pemmican as well as some travel biscuits and hard tack. He picked up two canteens and went out to the community well to fill them. He passed Guillaume on his way back.

"I must go and see Fèlicitè. Tell her we are leaving and make sure my nephews are well. Gather the supplies and roll them in our blankets so they will be easy to carry."

Archie nodded and hurried to do as he was asked.

* * *

The faint light of pre-dawn pearled the eastern horizon softening the harsh contours of the early winter landscape. A brisk wind swept down the Red River, billowing coats, and the coverings on the Red River ox carts. Guillaume checked to be sure Archie was still perched atop one of the carts before mounting his own sturdy little horse. Francois rode up beside him, well muffled against the chill.

"I see the English *garçon* is ready. Are you sure that is wise?" He eyed the boy with a speculative gaze.

"*Pourquoi*?" Guillaume swung around in surprise. "I can hardly leave him alone at the cabin."

Francois cleared his throat and edged his horse closer. "Have you considered that maybe he might be lying? Or perhaps he didn't see someone attack your sisters, but that it was him who was the culprit. Maybe he thought to merely rob them and not to commit murder."

Guillaume rubbed a mittened hand over his beard. "The thought has not occurred to me. But I suppose it is possible..."

"We will keep a close eye on him. I do not trust the *Anglais* as far as I can spit." Francois suited action to words.

The sound of wheels creaking and oxen lowing interrupted their conversation as the convoy of carts heaved into motion. Guillaume held his horse back until the last cart passed him. Riding at the tail of the procession wasn't as onerous now as it would be in the summer when heat and dust cloaked the end of the line of carts. He tucked the long ends of his scarf into his leather jacket, the north wind cutting into his side as the carts turned west along the Assiniboine River in the direction of Headingley where they would spend the first night of the journey. Hunching his shoulders and settling deeper into the saddle, he gave into his thoughts. The nephews were a constant worry, thank God for Fèlicitè who was more than willing to care for them. A tiny corner of his mind acknowledged the fact that she was more than a little interested in taking care of Guillaume as well. He shook his head; she was hardly more than a child. She is nineteen and more than old enough to be married, he argued with himself. And he needed to come up with a more permanent solution to the problem. Phaw! He spat over the horse's shoulder, time to think of that after he found the *saloud* who murdered his sisters and meted out his own form of justice.

The turn of thoughts brought his conversation with Francois back to the forefront of his mind. *Archie? Responsible for Marguerite and Marie-Anne's murders?* He kneed his mount further out on the flank of the convoy and sought the figure of the English boy now walking beside the fourth cart. It wouldn't be a bad idea to keep an eye on the young man. Was it coincidence that he just happened to be holed up in the shed on the night of the murders or was it more sinister than that? Instead of the tale he'd told Guillaume about one attacker, maybe there had been two assailants, or could the one attacker actually have been the boy himself? Judging by the way Archie handled the heavy pails of water and the items packed into the carts he was much stronger than he appeared. *I wonder how old he really is? I assumed him to be nine or ten, and he claims to be twelve, but he is scrawny and underfed, so perhaps he is much older than I thought.* Maudire! *I have enough to worry about without entertaining unfounded suspicions. And what of the silver button? If Archie was in possession of a silver button he would have sold or traded it for food or lodging not carried it around.*

Guillaume pushed the thoughts away but couldn't dismiss the lingering doubts. Archie was walking beside Francois holding onto a stirrup to help him keep up. From the way he kept glancing up at the rider, it was clear there was a conversation of sorts being carried on. A grim smile twisted Guillaume's lips. Trust Francois to try and winkle information out of the lad. He let his mount drop back behind the last cart and turned his attention to keeping an eye out for anything that might spell trouble.

* * *

The sun's last rays shot gold lances across the land, highlighting the scruff of clouds brushed across the darkening sky. The wind picked up with the descent of night, the first stars blinking into view against the deep royal blue stretching overhead. Guillaume's horse snorted and shook his head, quickening his pace as the ox carts ahead of them began pulling into a circle. When the last cart was in place, Guillaume stepped off the horse and went in search of Archie and Francois. He stripped the saddle and blankets off the beast and dropped them by the fire someone had already started. Archie appeared out of the gloom to take the horse and get it settled for the night. A task Guillaume was happy to have taken care of.

"A drink?" Francois joined him, offering a flask of whisky.

Guillaume took a long swallow and wiped his mouth with the back of his hand before returning the flask to his companion. "Did you learn anything interesting from our young friend?"

"Not as much as I would like. It was hard to pry much out of him."

"Perhaps you are right, and he is hiding something. I think I will go and help with the horse, see if I can get him to reveal anything." Guillaume left the ring of light thrown by the fire and made his way toward the livestock. He paused once he was away from the light to let his eyes adjust to the dark. It took only a moment to find the animal he was searching for. Long strides covered the distance, but the presence of another figure with Archie stopped him short.

Who can that be? It is not one of us, and how does Archie know the man? Slipping further into the shadows, Guillaume moved silently among the oxen who were more intent on eating than in his presence among them. He halted behind a team of oxen, hidden by the broad shoulders, close enough to hear the two men talking. *Merde!*

The taller man clasped Archie's hand. "Until we meet again, do not forget what I have said." He released the younger man's hand melted into the night.

Archie resumed stripping the horse's tack, visibly trembling even in the uncertain light. Guillaume retreated through the throng of animals and worked his way around to approach the boy from the direction of the fire.

"Archie! What is taking so long? Is Buck lame or injured in some way?" Guillaume ran a hand down the gelding's legs.

"N-n-no. He's fine. Guess I'm just more tired than I thought." Archie hobbled the horse before he began to gather up the gear.

Guillaume straightened up and regarded him. Who was that you were talking to a moment ago? His tone was casual, but his expression was not.

"What? Wasn't talkin' to no one." The boy kept his head down.

Guillaume laid a hand on his shoulder. "Do not lie to me. I saw you with someone just a few minutes ago. You either tell me who it was, or you can start walking back to Winnipeg."

His Adam's apple worked in his throat twice before he answered. "Someone my pa knew. From back home."

"How is he here? He is not with us and how did he know you were here?"

Archie nodded toward another fire some distance away. "He's with them trappers on their way to the Company with beaver pelts to trade."

"And how did he know you would be here?" Guillaume persisted.

Archie shrugged. "Didn't. I ran into him nosing around the oxen when I brought Buck over. Don't know how he recognized me, but he did. Says I look like me pa did at my age."

"And that is all? What did he want of you?" Guillaume hoped the youngster would confide in him. Francois suspicions nagged at the corner of his mind. Was there something more sinister going on that he was unaware of. And more importantly, did it have anything to do with his sisters.

"Nothin' really. I think he was maybe thinking of makin' off with one of the horses after we bedded down for the night. I told him we always set a night guard who shot first and asked questions later. Was that right?"

"It won't hurt, and I will be sure to let the others know. But you talked of nothing else?"

Archie shook his head, hitched the saddle up onto his hip, and let Guillaume take the blankets and bridle.

Guillaume let the conversation die with misgivings. He would need to pay more attention to where the boy went and if he wandered off on his own once the camp was settled for the night. Based on the bit of conversation he'd heard, there had been more to the exchange than the youngster was letting on. Maybe it was as innocent as it appeared on the surface and maybe not.

The pair returned to the fire where Archie went to help the man at the cook fire after setting the saddle down by their bedrolls. Guillaume followed him with his eyes and joined Francois.

"Something wrong, *mon ami*?" Francois looked up from where he was hunkered down on his heels holding a tin cup of coffee.

"Possibly." Guillaume dropped down beside him. "When I went to check on the horses, I discovered Archie talking to one of the trappers from the far fire."

"How is that? How did this trapper know the boy was here? I do not like this, not at all."

"I have to agree with you. When I questioned him, he was less than forthcoming."

"His explanation?" Francois spat a stream of tobacco juice.

"Claimed the trapper was a man who knew his father. Then he went on to say he thought the man was thinking of stealing a horse or two once our camp was asleep."

"Which might be true. But it seems more likely it was to distract you from asking about his relationship with this trapper, if that is indeed what he is."

"That has occurred to me as well. He seems innocent enough and my first instinct was to trust him when he came to me with what he saw, but now..."

"With what he *says* he saw. Do not forget there is only his word to back up his story. I think it would be wise if we both watch him to see if he reveals his true intentions." Francois got to his feet.

"I will be saddened if he proves to be a liar, but I would be foolish to not be cautious. Come, the rubaboo is ready, I can smell the stew from here." Guillaume unfolded his long frame from the ground.

"I've brought dinner. Stew and bannock, but the cook called it something weird." Archie juggled the tin plates, handing one to each man. "He called it rubaboo and *le galet*?"

Francois laughed. "*Imbècile Anglais!* It is exactly what you said."

Archie flushed in the firelight and dropped his gaze to his plate. He moved away from the two men and sat cross legged on one of the saddle blankets to eat.

Guillaume related Archie's suspicions about the trappers to the rest of the camp and they set up a guard rotation for the night. Though Archie volunteered to take a watch, Guillaume refused to let him based on his own suspicions.

The night was uneventful and pre-dawn saw the camp struck and the carts ready to roll across the frost glazed prairie.

*　*　*

Another two nights saw them past Headingley and in striking distance of White Horse Plain. The men gathered around the fire, eating, and sharing stories with much laughter and teasing. Guillaume accepted the skin of drink as it was passed, drinking enough to take the chill off his bones but not enough to impair his senses.

He kept a surreptitious eye on Archie, the young man was edgy and jumpy since the encounter the first night on the trail. Guillaume resisted the urge to shake the truth of the matter out of the English boy. There was more to the encounter than Archie was letting on, Guillaume's gut was rarely wrong when it came to understanding a situation.

He shook his head while anger rose in his chest. If only he had read the situation between Marguerite and the arrogant *saloud* she had welcomed into her life. Ashmore was at the root of the murders. Guillaume would bet his life on it. Not that the Englishman would dirty his hands to commit the deed himself, no, he would have employed one of his lackeys to take care of it for him. But who? His fingers found the silver button in his belt pouch, turning it over while contemplating possible suspects. The two Company men were top of his list. His gaze landed on Archie. His jaw clenched in frustration. The younger man seemed innocuous enough, but perhaps Francois was right and there was much more to the tale he told Guillaume than he was letting on.

As if Archie heard Guillaume's thoughts, he got to his feet and slipped out of the ring of firelight. Francois caught his friend's gaze across the fire and nodded toward the spot the Englishman disappeared. With a studied casualness, Guillaume unfolded his long body and moved to follow him, passing the skin of grog to the man beside him. He'd gotten no further than the outside of the ring of ox carts before a scream tore through the darkness. He whirled toward the sound, hand on his long knife, tensed for an attack. Eyes casting about in the faint starlight.

Archie burst into the firelight from the opposite direction he had disappeared. A fact Guillaume filed away for the moment.

Where had he gone in such a short time and why circle around the campsite if he only went to take care of necessary business. Long strides carried him back to the fire where a white-faced Archie was babbling.

"*Qu'as tu vu? Où êtes-vous allé?*" Guillaume shoved his way to Archie's side and gripped him by the shoulders.

The lips worked in the pale face but produced no recognizable sound other than a high whine. Francois handed Guillaume a full skin which he forced Archie to take a huge swallow from. The grog seemed to do the trick, coughing, and choking, he finally managed to speak.

"Ghost! I seen a ghost!" He swallowed hard and grabbed the skin of grog from Guillaume.

Someone tossed another piece of wood on the fire causing the flames to shoot up, while a few of the men threw glances over their shoulders into the surrounding expanse of dark prairie.

"*Des fantômes, non.*" Guillaume snorted in disgust. "Tell me why you went sneaking off? Who did you meet with?"

"N-n-n-no one, I swear." Archie shook his head so hard his hair came loose of its tie flying around his face.

"What did this ghost of yours look like?" Angus, the man in charge of the convoy of ox carts broke into the conversation.

Archie gulped and glanced into the night. "A big white thing, or maybe it was grey...huge. It was huge, with long hair whipping around it. Me Irish gram would call it a pooka, or she'd say it was Goath, the wind horse of the Tuatha de Dannan."

Laugher rippled through the men.

"Who calls a horse 'gwee'? What kinda name is that?" Francois ridiculed him.

Archie drew himself up as tall as his five-foot-four stature would allow. "It don't pay to speak ill of the Good Folk," he warned.

Guillaume snorted and took a swig of grog.

"Maybe he saw the ghost horse of the plains?" Angus moved out of the light to peer into the darkness.

"You talkin' about that Injun horse what's supposed to hang around these here parts?" one of the other men joined the conversation.

"Could be." Angus returned to the fire. "Ain't nothing out there now." He settled himself by the fire.

"What do you know of this white horse?" Hiram, one of the Scotsmen with the convoy asked. "I sure as hell don't want to be meetin' up with any *each-uisge* out here. Might be they could live in the Assiniboine."

"What in the name of God is an aughisky?" One of the Metis snorted.

"Water horse," Hiram said. "Mean creatures they be. Offer to take a man for a ride, then once you're on his back you can't get off and the bastard jumps back in the river or any water nearby and drowns you."

He shivered and made the old ward against evil with the fingers of his left hand.

"It ain't no water horse. Iffen you really want to hear the tale then set back down and I'll tell ya." Angus waved a hand at the abandoned area around the fire.

The group settled down, passing the skin among them again. Guillaume made sure he was within reaching distance of Archie. Damned if he'd let the fool go wandering off again.

Phillipe leaned back against his saddle propped up to support his back and caught the gaze of everyone around the fire.

"It's not a pretty tale, I'm afraid." He stared up at the stars for a long moment and seemed to compose himself before he began. "And this is how it was. Back in the sixteen-nineties, there was this Assiniboine chief who had a beautiful daughter. There were two chiefs what wanted to take her in what we would call marriage. One of 'em was a Sioux from Devil's Lake, the other a Cree from Lake Winnipegosis. The general thought was the Sioux would be the one chosen by the girl's father as the Sioux were allies to the Assiniboine and already related by other means. The Cree were traditional enemies of the Assiniboine. But," he paused to sweep his gaze around the circle of men, "the Cree chief offered the Assiniboine chief a gift in order to sway his choice. A huge white horse, a *Blanco Diablo* one of the famous Mexican breed. That's white devil in the Spanish tongue. This horse was reported to be strong and sturdy and nimble, and it was said he could outrun and outlast any other horse, all the while going three or four days longer than any other horse without food or water. 'A course, ain't no one today who can say aye or nay to that boast. Anyways, the horse was the clincher. The girl's father chose the Cree chief and took possession of the magnificent stallion. No doubt imagining how that horse would improve his herd of ponies.

His choice of mate for his daughter was not a popular one, either with his own people or with the Sioux. The Assiniboine medicine man was outraged as it was his duty to send the word of rejection to the Sioux chief. He shouted at the Assiniboine chief accusing him of making peace with the enemies of their forefathers and bringing disgrace on the Assiniboine by mingling their blood with their sworn foes. His protests did no good, the Assiniboine chief really wanted that white horse for his own.

The horse along with other gifts were presented and the Cree chief claimed the girl. A huge feast along with much merrymaking ensued. However during the celebrations a huge cloud of dust was observed on the horizon, coming closer and closer. An alarm was raised, because of course, it was the rejected Sioux chief coming to avenge the insult he had been given.

The Sioux war party attacked the Assiniboine gathering on the wedding night. In fear for their lives, the Cree chief and the Assiniboine woman ran and caught two horses. She on the famed white stallion, the Cree on a grey horse. Iffen you ask me, they should have chosen a bay or even a chestnut to run away on. Even in the dark, white and grey horses are easy to spot and sure enough the Sioux saw them and took off after them.

The white stallion could have outpaced the Sioux easily if the tales are to be believed, but the story has it that she held the horse back so the Cree chief could keep up. It wasn't the smartest thing she ever did, but who knows what any woman is thinking? The Sioux caught them just about where we're camped tonight. Even though the Sioux originally wanted to have the Assiniboine girl join their tribe, their rage was too great. They sent volley after volley of arrows at the cornered couple and killed them both. The Sioux managed to capture the grey horse, perhaps in the poor light they thought they'd caught the magnificent white horse. But the stallion escaped and there were stories for years about travellers seeing him wandering the nearby plains, but never near enough to catch or even be sure it was him." Angus took a long drink of grog, then spat and rubbed his hands together. "The tale doesn't end there though. Legend has it that the soul of the girl joined with the white stallion when she died, and it is her who haunts the plains here abouts in the skin of the horse. So maybe what the *sassenach* here saw tonight was the ghost of the girl embodied in the famous white horse. This here area used to be called *Coteau de Festin* because it's been a gatherin' place for the Injuns for longer than anyone can remember." He got to his feet. "That's me tale for the night. Time to turn in."

The rest of the men made ready for sleep, Guillaume had early guard duty and made sure to keep Archie with him. Maybe after his earlier scare and the ghost story, not to mention his exhaustion, the younger man could be persuaded to reveal whatever secrets Guillaume was sure he was keeping.

Chapter Seven

Guard duty passed with no more conversation from Archie other than noncommittal one word replies or grunts. Disgusted, Guillaume relinquished his duty to the next man and returned to the dying fire to roll up in his blankets. The pearl grey light of false dawn found him crusty eyed and unrested. Every time Archie moved, Guillaume started out of his doze to make sure he wasn't sneaking off again. The group of what he assumed were buffalo hunters and trappers was still visible by their fire a mile or so to the north-west of them. It didn't escape his notice that Archie frequently looked in that direction, with fear and something Guillaume struggled to identify in his expression. The English boy hadn't learned the valuable lesson of hiding his emotions when he thought he was unobserved. A fact Guillaume was most thankful for.

The camp roused and set about the task of moving on. They should reach the buffalo hunters camp by evening. Guillaume resolved to seek out the man he'd seen with Archie and find out what was going on between the two. Whatever it was, it didn't seem to be friendly, regardless of Archie's claims the man was a friend of his deceased father. Rising sun found them on the move, Guillaume astride his horse with an eye on Archie who was getting a lesson in driving one of the Red River carts. He breathed a sigh of relief, that should keep the young man occupied and out of trouble. A load of responsibility lifted from his shoulders, he urged his horse into a lope and joined Francois riding on the north flank of the line of carts.

"What do you make of the English boy and the man from the other group headed in the same direction as we are?" Guillaume nodded toward the faint haze of dust to the north of their path.

"It seems odd. You say he told you the man is a friend of his father?"

"*Oui*, but from what I saw, and from how he behaved, I wouldn't say the encounter was friendly."

"Maybe the father owes this man something and he thinks he can get if from the son?" Francois ventured a guess.

"*C'est possible*, I can get no information from the boy. But I think that will have to change very soon."

"And, if as I suspect, your Archie had something to do with what happened to Marguerite and Marie Anne, then perhaps, this buffalo hunter or trapper or whatever he is, may be involved too."

"*Merde!* This just keeps getting more complicated. I don't know what to think anymore."

"I think, *mon ami,* that you must get that young man to reveal whatever it is he is hiding. And soon."

"I have to agree with you." Guillaume scrubbed a hand over his bearded face. He liked Archie, felt sorry for him, it was hard to believe he could be involved in anything to do with the murders. Still, Francois did make some very interesting points that couldn't be ignored.

Their arrival at the buffalo camp was greeted with much enthusiasm. The piles of buffalo hides were loaded onto the carts once the incoming supplies were unloaded. Spirits were high as the two groups gathered around the fire in the circle of the ox carts. The women were busy with the tasks of producing food for the men as well as caring for the production of pemican and the curing of the newest buffalo hides. Guillaume spared them a moment; glad he was a man and not required to bear the burden of caring for the camp and the men.

It was late when he left the circle of firelight to seek his bed roll. As he approached the place where he'd left Archie in charge of setting up their bedrolls and storing their equipment, he noted the boy's bed roll wasn't occupied.

"Where the hell is he? I told him to watch our belongings." Guillaume tamped down his anger. It had been a long day and all he wanted was to lie beneath the stars and let the stars of the Fisher lead him into sleep. The whites called the Fisher constellation the Great Bear or the Big Dipper, but Guillaume's Cree mother taught him the traditional name and he adhered to her teachings in all things.

However, this wasn't solving the mystery of where the English boy was. He moved toward where the horses and oxen were grazing. Giving Archie the benefit of the doubt, perhaps he heard something bothering the animals. Or perhaps not…

Nearing the clump of odd-shaped shadows he identified as the livestock, Guillaume slowed his steps. Hushed voices reached his ears. One he recognized as Archie, but the other was a rough Scottish burr. Was this the stranger for earlier, the one travelling with the other camp? Silently, he slipped closer, working his way into the herd without disturbing the horses or oxen. Reaching a vantage point where he could hear the harsh whispers and by looking between the horses see a little of what was transpiring.

A tall, bearded man dressed in well used buckskins, a battered hat pulled low over his face and a rifle in his hand had his other hand wrapped in the front of Archie's shirt. Even in the gloom the English boy's face was stark and pale, eyes wide and black as pitch in the shadows. Guillaume shifted closer, intent on figuring out once and for all what the connection between the two was.

"Yer pa owed me, so now you owes me," the Scotsman snarled. "I want what's owed me and I want it now." He gave the boy a hard shake.

"I ain't got nothin' to give you," Archie's voice wavered. "I don't know nothin' about what Pa owed you. He never said anythin' to me about owing nobody."

"Ain't my problem what yer pa said or didn't say. Ya owe me, and ya better not ever spill your guts about what else you know, if you know what's good fer ya."

"I don't know nothin'." Archie tried to pry the man's hand off his shirt.

"That's right. Ya don't know nothin' about what happened that night. Whatever it is ya think ya know, ya'd best fergit it."

Guillaume's heart quickened. What night was the man referring to? The night Marguerite and Marie-Anne were murdered? Or a different night and something else all together. Before the night was out, Archie was going to tell him everything he knew, one way or another.

"I don't know nothin' to fergit. I wasn't there."

"Yer pa tell ye something about it, then? What went down that night in Winnipeg?"

Guillaume shifted forward a step before he stopped himself. Better to hear what there was to hear before he revealed his presence. Perhaps he could finish this here and now, avenge his sisters without the interference of the Company or anyone else.

"He didn't say nothin'. He was hurt bad when he came back to the squat that last night. I was too scairt to ask him who beat him or why." Archie swallowed hard, breath rushing harsh from his mouth.

The Scotsman thrust him away and spat on the ground beside where he sprawled almost under the hooves of the nearest horses. "Just ya be rememberin' that. Ya don't know nothin' about nothin'." He strode away into the night. Moments later the sound of galloping hooves echoed in the silence.

Archie lay where he'd fallen for a long moment before raising himself on his elbows and looking in the direction the man disappeared. He muffled a squeal and scrambled backward like a crab when Guillaume stepped out from the herd.

"You want to tell me what that was all about?" His voice left no question that he would have the answer whether Archie was inclined to tell him or not. Reaching down he hauled the boy to his feet. Guillaume kept a hand on his arm, taking in the panicked expression on Archie's face and the way his gaze darted about as if seeking an escape route.

"Where would you run to? No one to protect you out there and that Scotsman will be lookin' for you. I'm thinkin' if you don't give him what he wants he'll take great pleasure in beating it out of your hide."

Archie sagged in the bigger man's grip, all the fight draining out of him. Guillaume dragged him away from the herd, moving closer to the camp in case he needed to call on Francois for assistance. Sitting cross-legged on the prairie he pulled the boy down with him. "Now talk. I want all of it, and if I think you're lying to me, then you're on your own again. I won't abide a liar. It is your choice, *mon ami.*"

The rustle of the boy's clothing betrayed the trembling of his body, belying the firmness of his clenched jaw. Archie kept his head down, refusing to meet Guillaume's gaze. After a few minutes of silence, Guillaume decided it was time to call his bluff. With a sigh, he levered himself to his feet and looked down at the boy.

"I wish you luck, you will most certainly need it." He turned on his heel and made to walk back toward the camp where the bedrolls and equipment were waiting.

"Wait." Archie's hand gripped Guillaume's buckskins.

"I am tired of waiting. If you are ready to talk, I may still be willing to listen." Guillaume sank back to the short grass covering the prairie.

Archie gulped noisily and shredded a stalk of grass in his fingers.

"I am waiting," Guillaume prompted him. "Who is that man?"

"I don't know his name. My pa met him and some other men on the ship and then we travelled with them all the way to Winnipeg. I didn't like any of them." He shuddered. "One of 'em was too friendly by half. Always touchin' me when Pa weren't around."

"Did he hurt you?" Guillaume's voice was gentler now.

Archie shook his head. "I learned how to keep away from him when no one was around."

"What did your pa do with them?"

"Don't know for sure. They usta go off at night, after I was supposed to be asleep and come back just before the sun come up."

"You don't know what they did when they were gone?"

"They talked about wimmen, some. And sometimes, they'd come back with stuff."

"Like what stuff?"

"Food usually. But sometimes, it were furs, or those Company bits of copper, almost always there'd be grog they called it. I didn't like it when they got drunk. Scairt me."

"Why does that man think your pa owes him something?"

Archie shrugged and shook his head. "Don't know. I don't know nothin' about that."

"Did they play cards or gamble. Did your pa gamble with them?"

"Maybe some? I didn't pay much mind to what they did as long as they weren't botherin' me."

"What night is the man threatening you about? What night was that?" Guillaume fought to keep his voice steady. So close, maybe so close.

"I think it's the night my pa got hurt. Don't know for sure. All's I know is Pa came back from one of them long nights all bashed up. Wouldn't say what happened, just lay down. Told me to be a good boy and get him somethin' to eat." Archie lapsed into silence, his throat working.

"What happened."

He shrugged. "I went to try and find something to eat in the garbage behind the saloon, when I got back...when I got back Pa wouldn't wake up. I shook him and shook him, but he wouldn't wake up."

Guillaume put a hand on the boy's shoulder. "What happened to him when he wouldn't wake up?"

Archie glanced at him from the side of his eyes. "He was dead. I figured that much out myself. Then two of the men came 'round lookin' for him and they took him away. I tried to follow them. I mean it was my pa they was takin' somewheres. But they run me off and I never did find out what they did with him. Threw him in the river I reckon." His shoulders slumped and shook with quiet tears.

"Are any of those men the one you said you saw when you were hiding in the shed the night my sisters were murdered," Guillaume's voice was underlaid with steel. He slid his hand under the boy's chin and forced him to meet his gaze.

"What! No!" His eyes were wide with terror. "No!"

"Do not lie to me. If one of them is the man you saw that night I will deal with them, I assure you."

"No, it wasn't one of them. The man I saw was smaller and not so heavy. He smelled clean, not like them at all."

"Now that is an interesting bit of information you never told me. You're sure the person you saw smelled clean?"

"Yes, I'm sure. After living without a way to keep clean and smelling like a pig pen, you notice things like that. I just never thought it would be something important that you would want to know. Me Ma would scald me arse if she'd ever seen the way I was when you took me in."

"If you remember anything else about that night, no matter how small, be sure to tell me. Now, I think we will turn in for the night and tomorrow I will go and seek out this man who is bothering you and see what he has to say for himself."

Archie scrambled to his feet. "You won't make me go with him, will you? You won't let him take me?"

Guillaume got to his feet. "Why would I do that?"

"He said I owed him and iffen I couldn't pay him then he said I was endendered to him. He could make me work for him and do whatever he said until he decided I paid him off." He hesitated. "I don't think I'd ever be able to pay him what he wants."

Guillaume shook his head. "You mean indentured? He can't do that, and he won't. You can stop worrying about that. Francois and I will pay the other camp a visit tomorrow. Come, let's get some sleep. Morning comes early."

Side by side they made their way back to their bedrolls. Francois was sitting leaning on his saddle chewing on some pemican. He raised his eyebrow at Guillaume who signalled with his hand he would explain later.

Once he was sure Archie was asleep, he crouched close to his friend. "Our little friend had another visit from the stranger with the other camp. It was not a pleasant encounter. Come, I'll explain more as we go." Guillaume straightened and shifted the large knife at his belt.

Francois got to his feet and followed him out of the ring of firelight. "What are you planning?" He fell into step beside his friend as they bypassed the grazing horses.

Guillaume glanced at the stars to gauge the time. "Walking will suit best, I think. I want to catch the *saloud* unawares and hopefully get him away from the others without raising an alarm. He may have answers for me, and if nothing else he will either confirm or prove false Archie's stories."

"What did the boy tell you?" Keeping their voices hushed the two men slipped across the shadowed prairie, keeping to the lower sots where the ground rolled slightly.

Guillaume related the information Archie had given him. "He seemed genuinely scared, but as you pointed out, what do I really know about him?"

"Can you recognize the man in the dark? How well did you see him?"

"*Oui*, he is not wearing buckskins, and his shirt is a bright plaid. They appear to still be awake, and if he is talking, I will certainly recognize the voice" Guillaume nodded toward the ring of men drinking around the far fire.

Silent now, the two men moved closer, stopping outside the flickering light. They hunkered down in a shallow hollow behind a bit of scraggly bush that betrayed the presence of water beneath the soil. Guillaume kept an eye on the journey of the stars overhead and estimated it was past midnight. He caught his breath and met Francois' gaze in the starlight when a man rose and headed off into the dark presumably to take care of business. Francois raised an eyebrow in question, and Guillaume nodded in return.

Together, they slipped around the light toward where the man disappeared. The man staggered a little while he fumbled with his flies. One swift move brought Guillaume up behind him, knife to the man's throat and a hand across his mouth and nose. A surprised gurgle was all that emerged before Francois stepped in front of the pair and stunned the man with the hilt of his skinning knife. Guillaume took the weight and together they half-dragged-half-carried the man farther away from the camp.

They discovered a small swale leading down toward the Assiniboine River and slid down the side of the gully. Taking the rawhide thongs from his belt Guillaume bound the man's hands and feet before stuffing a rag into his mouth. "Now we wait." He sat back on his heels. Archie was right, the man did stink. A quick rummage through the man's clothing revealed no trace of anything of value, let alone anything silver. He glanced up at Francois who perched at the lip of the swale watching for any movement from the stranger's camp. "It seems unlikely this man would be in possession of a silver button. Not unless he somehow managed to steal just one button from someone. Still, we will wait for him to come around and he will answer my questions."

Francois nodded. "No movement," he whispered.

Orion moved a finger's width in the sky before a groan emerged from the prone figure. Guillaume leaned closer when the man's eyes flickered open, blinked, and then widened in terror. He struggled a moment against his bonds before subsiding, sweat popping out on his forehead. The thin chest rose and fell in rapid motions under the dirty plaid shirt.

Francois stayed where he was, dividing his attention between the camp and Guillaume. Placing the big knife against the man's throat, Guillaume leaned down, putting enough pressure on the blade to draw a trickle of blood. The man froze and emitted strangled noises behind the gag.

"I have questions and you have the answers, I believe. And you will answer me, make no mistake. I will remove the gag and you will talk, quietly. If you make any move to escape or call for help, I will slit your throat. *Comprende*?"

The man blinked, his captor relaxed the tension on the blade a fraction allowing the man a tiny nod of acceptance. Guillaume glanced up at Francois, who gave the all clear signal, then pulled the rag out of the man's mouth.

"Who are ye? What do ye want wi' me?" His voice was harsh and dry.

"I ask the questions," Guillaume warned, keeping the knife at the man's throat.

"What do you know about the murder of the two Metis women that were found by the river recently?"

"I don't know nothin' about them women." His eyes flicked wildly from side to side.

"I think you lie." The blade pressed a little harder into the side of his neck. "Surely, you have heard something..." A thread of blood ran down his neck and pooled by his collarbone.

The man swallowed, careful of the blade. "Okay, yeah I might a heard some talk at O'Lone's."

"What talk?"

"Wal, there was them two Company men what went after a couple a Frenchies looking for some fun, but they let 'em go. Came back to the saloon all pissed off about them having some kinda note from a big shot about fetching somethin' for him from Shultz's and they didn't wanna risk getting in trouble. Why'd ya care? They was just some French Half-Breeds, prob'ly a couple of thrown away whores. There's lots of them Frenchies what got booted out by the English when they brought their fancy English ladies over and wed 'em in church." He trailed off, perhaps suddenly realizing the man with the knife at his throat was also a French Half-Breed. "I don't know for sure though, I never had anything to do with anythin'. Just what I heard after they came back..."

"Those women were my sisters and considered themselves married *à la façon du pays,* according to the custom of the country, in your words. You *Anglais* make me sick. Did those Company men harm those women?"

"No, no. I swear it."

Guillaume placed a knee on the man's chest and pressed hard. "If I find you have lied to me, I will hunt you down. Have no doubt." He paused to control the frustration roiling in his gut. A bit more information, but ultimately a dead end in his search to find the murderer. This piece of *merde* was a waste of time in that regard. However... "Now, let us speak of the young English boy you have been harassing. What is it you want with him?"

The man's eyes widened, then flicked about, looking anywhere except at Guillaume. The knife released another flow of blood down his neck while the knee on his chest forced the breath from his lungs. "What boy?" He gave it one last desperate attempt at deceit.

"You know which boy. Speak before I lose patience..."

"Met him and his pa on the ship comin' from Liverpool. Made an arrangement with the man, took him into our employ, so to speak."

"And...." The knee pressed harder.

"Okay, okay. We had a deal goin', a good deal. But the old man got anxious, worried about gettin' caught. Then he screwed up, big time and we had ta, you know, teach him a lesson. Keep him in line…"

"But you went too far, and he died. Isn't that right?"

"I guess. Don't know. He just disappeared. Figured he'd moved on, maybe headed down to Saint Boniface or Saint Cloud."

"So why hunt down the boy? Wouldn't you have thought he would have gone with his father?"

"Don't know, don't care. I saw the whelp and thought I'd just see if I could squeeze out of 'em where his pa hid what he stole fer us. If his pa is really dead, then the boy owes us. Sins of the father and all that."

"I think not," Guillaume growled. "Did the boy steal for you too? Or just the father?"

"Don't know if he helped or not. Don't care. Just want what's owed me." The tone grew belligerent in spite of the knife at his neck.

"You," Guillaume leaned on his knee and was pleased to feel ribs break, "are owed nothing. You will not bother the boy again or you will answer to me." He paused. "That is if I decide to let you live this night. Francois?" He raised his head to check with his friend.

"All quiet," Francois reported.

"*Bien.*" He turned his attention back to the prone man. "This is what we will do. You will forget you ever knew the English boy or his father. You will leave the village of Winnipeg and surroundings. You will mention this evening to no one, and you will forget you ever saw me. *Comprende?* Understand?”

“Yeah, yeah, okay.” The man’s voice was thin and breathless as he tried to speak and breathe without moving his damaged ribs.

“*Bien.*” Guillaume stuffed the rag back in the man’s mouth and rose. “If you are lucky your friends will come and look for you in the morning. If not...” He shrugged and bounded up the short slope to join Francois.

“An interesting conversation,” Francois observed.

“It seems the boy was telling the truth as far as that was concerned. About the night my sisters died...I’m not so sure he has told me everything. *Maintenant*, we need to get back.”

Two shadows drifted across the dark prairie, skirting the other campfire and keeping as low as possible to disguise their movements across the landscape. After checking their livestock, the two men rolled themselves in their blankets. Soft snores came from Francois’ bedroll while Guillaume watched the pace of the stars across the heavens, one eye on Archie and one ear open for sounds of excitement from the other camp.

Chapter Eight

Four days travel found them back home. After assisting with unloading the buffalo hides and other furs, Guillaume stopped to check the welfare of his nephews with Fèlicitè.

"Guillaume!" Fèlicitè swung the door open wide. "Look *bèbès*, it is your *oncle*!" She stepped aside to allow him to enter and be mobbed by the two boys. Alexandre pulled back first while Ètienne continued to cling to his uncle's buckskin clad legs.

"Can we go home now?" Alexandre scuffed the toe of his moccasin on the wide planked floor.

"For now, *oui*. We will go home. But you must both behave, and you must listen to Archie, here if I have to leave you with him sometimes. *Comprende*?"

Archie hovered just inside the doorway, head down. Alexandre regarded the English boy with dubious concern, but he nodded. Ètienne peeked at Archie before running to hide his face in Fèlicitè's skirts.

"*Non*, don't like him. Want to stay here."

Fèlicitè ran a hand over his hair, met Guillaume's gaze over his head, and lifted a shoulder. "It is no trouble. He can stay if you wish."

Guillaume crossed the floor and scooped his nephew up in his arms. "Come home with me. We are family and belong together." He freed one hand and gripped the young woman's in thanks. "I don't know what I would do without you, *mon ami*. I hope these *bonnehommes* were not too much of a burden along with your own work."

Fèlicitè ducked her head for a moment before looking up, a brilliant smile on her face. "I enjoy having them. It's not like I have any of my own to care for."

He detected a bitter tinge to her last words. At nineteen, almost twenty, many women her age already had children at their skirts. Guillaume met her gaze with a smile of his own, seeing her in a new light for the first time.

"I'm sure it won't be long before you have a fine family of your own." He took Alexandre's hand in his and shifted Ètienne to a more secure position on his hip. "You are welcome to visit anytime you wish, Fèlicitè. I would appreciate your help again when I have to be away." He moved toward the door and turned as a thought came to him. What have you heard of this new provisional government Grant and Riel are keen to implement? I have heard nothing since I have been gone."

She shook her head and frowned. "There is talk of violence by some, but Riel seems to be not in favour of bloodshed. Although Grant is the president in name, it seems that Louis is the real leader who most are listening to. I heard that the Canadian government in Upper Canada has offered the Hudson's Bay Company a lot of money for control of Rupert's Land. Already there has been some trouble with surveyor men coming onto our farms uninvited and being run off. It is troubling and it seems that Prime Minister man, Mister Macdonald cares nothing for us who have been here for years and intends to take our land from us and give it to his friends. Grant and Riel are working to protect the rights of the French Half-Breeds at least, the English ones seem content to wait and see what happens."

"That is troubling. There is a meeting tomorrow night, I think it will be in our best interests if I attend. Please ask your papa to come by later tonight. I thank you again for your help." He dipped his head in acknowledgement and herded his little brood out the door.

"Is there gonna be trouble?" Archie fell into step beside him. "There were riots back home in Liverpool a while back and it scared me Ma so bad she wouldn't let me out of her sight."

"Nothing for you to worry about. You keep out of trouble in the village when you're not minding the boys and when you are out and about be sure to keep your ears open for anything that might help me find the *saloud*

I am seeking." He was careful not to mention his sisters' names or the murders while Ètienne and Alexandre were within earshot. The poor *bèbès* had been through enough without reminding them of the loss. There was still a gaping hole in his own heart that only his rage and determination to avenge his sisters kept from overwhelming him.

Opening the door to his cabin, he was surprised to find a fire already lit and a crockery bean pot on the table covered with a thick cloth. The savoury scent of Rubaboo rising in the steam seeping through the cloth welcomed him home. He set Ètienne down and shut the door.

"Fèlicitè and I came here earlier when she heard you were coming home today, and we tidied up and then brought our supper." Alexandre waved a proud hand around the cabin. "I like her. Can she come and live with us, *oncle*? I know she would like to."

Guillaume grinned to hide the quick spurt of embarrassment and something else. "Why would Fèlicitè wish to leave her own home to come and live with us? Ours is much smaller than where she lives now." He moved to light the oil lamp and then shake out the blankets on the beds.

"We already did that," Alexandre informed him. He looked up at Guillaume, appearing undecided about something. A tiny bob of his head indicated he'd come to some decision. "I think Fèlicitè would like to come and live with us. I heard her talking to her friend when we were supposed to be sleeping. She thinks you are very handsome and some other stuff I don't remember. But she did say she would be happy if you were to speak with her papa." He paused and frowned. "But I don't understand why, because you speak with her papa all the time and that doesn't make her happy…"

Guillaume coughed and ducked his head to hide his expression from his nephew. An interesting thought, and it would solve many problems. But was that a good enough reason to make such a commitment?

"Come, let's see about tasting this Rubaboo and then getting you two bonnehommes settled."

* * *

The boys were asleep, finally, and Archie was curled up by the fire struggling to comprehend the simple math problems Guillaume set for him. A brief rap announced Baptiste's arrival before the door opened. Fèlicitè's father joined his friend, taking the other chair by the hearth.

"All is well out at the camp? Fèlicitè said you brought back many robes and furs."

"*Oui*, the camp is fine. I had a bit of trouble with some trappers from another camp. Englishmen who had some issues with the boy there." He tipped his head toward where Archie frowned at the

139

scrapped hide trying to make sense of the addition and subtraction calculations.

"Ahh, you settled it to your satisfaction?"

Guillaume nodded. "But tell me what is happening with this annexation by Canada nonsense. The Company has managed Rupert's Land quite satisfactorily for as long as I can remember. What benefit is it to us to have the Canadians come in, and if the rumours are true, take our land from us to give to their own kind."

Baptiste scrubbed a hand over his beard. "It worries me, to be sure. We have already had to run off some of their so-called surveyors who are trying to impose their odd square shaped plots on us. They are running roughshod over our longer thin plots which allow everyone access to the river and water for the livestock and living. So far, we have been successful, but there is talk of them sending in more soldiers from Upper Canada. I like this man MacDonald not at all. He knows nothing of us or how things are here in Rupert's Land and yet he believes he has the right to impose his will on us."

"Do you support the idea of this provisional government that Grant and Riel are proposing? From what I have heard, and Fèlicitè seemed to confirm when I spoke with her earlier, Riel is against violence and will only resort to it as a last resort to force the Canadians to treat us fairly. Is it true the English Half-Breeds are not in support even though they could lose their land as well as us?"

Baptiste shook his head. "I don't understand them, but that is how things stand I'm afraid." He took a drink from the skin Guillaume offered him. "Are you coming to the meeting tomorrow night?"

"*Oui,* I think it is in our best interest to hear what the group has to say and how they plan to move forward. I understand Hugh O'Lone is a supporter."

"He is, *oui.* Why are you interested in him in particular?"

"I am hoping he will have heard gossip or bragging in the saloon about the murder of my sisters. Men tend to boast about such things to their friends when they are drinking."

"*Entrè,*" Guillaume responded to a tap on the door.

"I heard you were back, bonne soirèe, Baptiste." Pierre joined the men by the fire, taking a seat on the long bench to the side. "A good trip?"

"Fair enough," Guillaume allowed. He leaned forward, elbows on his knees. "What have you heard while I've been away? I have learned nothing of importance on the trail. Have you been keeping an eye out for anyone missing a silver button on their coats?"

Pierre sighed and sat back on the bench. "Of the silver button, nothing. Most of the talk, and what is being printed in the paper, is focused on the Company relinquishing control of Rupert's Land to Canada. I did overhear a few of the English ladies chatting when I was at Schutlz's drug store to buy tobacco. They all seemed to be in accord that the sooner the country wives were gone and forgotten about the better it would be. They expressed dislike and embarrassment for having to put up with children, dirty urchins they called them, running up and calling the women's husbands their fathers. One of them even suggested they ask their respective husbands to take care of the matter."

"Take care of the matter?" Guillaume glowered and clenched his hands. "Take care of them how?"

"That they didn't say, *mon ami*. But they did make it sound a somewhat permanent solution to their supposed problem." Pierre shook his head. "It was all I could do not to take them to task. Calling my sweet Marie-Anne a whore…"

"A good thing it was you and not me who overheard this. Miles Ashmore would like nothing more than to clap me in jail and haul me up before the quarterly courts, and I don't believe I could have kept my temper hearing such terrible things about my sisters."

"Peace, Guillaume." Baptiste laid a hand on his arm. "Perhaps we need to look further than the Company men and the saloon for your murderer."

Guillaume bolted upright and looked from Pierre to Baptiste. "You are suggesting one of the richer Englishmen? Perhaps Miles Ashmore is behind this. But I have trouble believing that of him. I know he genuinely cared for Marguerite and the boys, even though I never trusted him."

"Times change," Pierre reminded him. "Look how many of our women are returning to their father's cabin after being discarded like so much offal. Because they are not elegant enough, not well bred enough, which means they are not full-blooded Englishwomen."

"And thank God for that," Baptiste said. "I can't imagine one of those delicate *Anglais* as my wife and helpmate." He spat into the fire. "Phaah, they are useless, perhaps pretty to look at in a pale sort of way, but not suited to the real life of living here. I don't understand what those foolish men see in them."

Pierre snorted. "They see them as status symbols, as proof of their perceived high standing in the community. They parade them around on their arms like a trophy at their soirèes and on Sundays as they congregate in their church."

Guillaume leaned back and rubbed his chin. "It makes sense in a way, the silver button does suggest it was someone with a bit of coin who attacked them. Something to look into."

"Go careful. Tensions are high already between us and the English. Tempers are flaring and it is all Riel and Grant can do to keep things under control. I fear there will be some action soon against the Canadian annexation. Men are worried about losing their land and homes and none of us are willing to go quietly." Baptiste shook his grizzled head.

The men spoke of other things for a while longer before leaving to return to their own homes. They agreed to get together before going to Riel's meeting the next night.

Chapter Nine

The four men entered the community hall, the frowsty air redolent of unwashed bodies, tobacco smoke, wet wool and leather mixed with the wood smoke from the fire. Francois and Baptiste moved off to speak with Xavier Pagèe and Paul Proulx. Guillaume worked his way through the knots of men, Pierre at his side. He scanned the room searching for Hugh O'Lone in particular.

"Will! I was hoping you would be here tonight." Hugh clapped Guillaume on the shoulder.

"Ah, Hugh. I was hoping to speak with you about something." He shrugged off O'Lone's anglicization of his name, as always. "Is there something in particular you wanted to see me about?"

"I have some information I think you may find interesting. But later, after this is over." He paused and scowled. "That bastard Orangeman Thomas Scott is stirrin' things up with the help of Mair and Schultz, those black devils." O'Lone's American accent was still strong, the harsh twang of his childhood in Hell's Kitchen, New York had left its mark.

The assembled men turned their attention to Ambrose Lèpine who called the meeting to order. The main topic of conversation and controversy was the proposed List of Rights which Riel, with his legal and political knowledge, drafted with the support of the priests Richot and Dugas. He sought to make sure that everyone's rights were protected. The English speakers, old settlers, new arrivals, along with the Half-Breeds — both French and English, Mètis, Indians and American were all included under Riel's umbrella of List of Rights.

Riel stood to speak. "I propose a totally bilingual community. This is not a document of surrender or submission. This is the demand of an equal people entering Confederation. We are asking nothing more than what has been granted to the people of Nova Scotia and New Brunswick."

There was some rustle of clothing and shuffling of feet along with a muted ripple of conversation. Riel cleared his throat and accepted the sheaf of paper that O'Donoghue, a prominent member of the Provisional Government which Cuthbert Grant and Louis Riel seemed to be the head of, handed him. Riel bowed his shaggy head and scanned the paper in the flickering light before looking up and staring at the gathered men with his dark piercing gaze.

"This is the List of Rights that we will demand of William McDougall and his chief

Prime Minister MacDonald," Riel began, pausing after each item in the list. "One. That the people have the right to elect their own Legislature.

Two. That the Legislature have the power to pass all laws local to the Territory over the veto of the Executive by a two-thirds vote.

Three. That no action of the Dominion Parliament (local to the Territory) be binding on the people sanctioned by the Legislature of the Territory.

Four. That all sheriffs, magistrates, constables, school commissioners, etc. be elected by the people.

Five. A free homestead and pre-emption land law.

Six. That the portion of the public lands be appropriated to the benefit of the schools, the building of bridges, roads, and public buildings.

Seven. That it be guaranteed to connect Winnipeg by rail, with the nearest line of railroad, within a term of five years; the land grant to be subject to the Local Legislature.

Eight. That for the term of four years all military, civil, and municipal expenses be paid out of the Dominion funds.

Nine. That the military be composed of the inhabitants now existing in the Territory.

Ten. That the English and French languages be common in the Legislature and Courts, and that all public documents and acts of the legislature be published in both languages.

Eleven. That the Judge of the Supreme Court speak the English and French languages.

Twelve. That the Treaties be concluded and ratified between the Dominion Government and the several tribes of Indians in the Territory to ensure peace on the frontier.

Thirteen. That we have a fair and full representation in the Canadian Parliament.

Fourteen. That all privileges, customs, and usages existing at the time of the transfer be respected.

He concluded and ran his powerful gaze over the assembly once more. " One thing that we must determine, is if McDougall has the authority to accept our List of Rights. If he does not, he must obtain, and prove he has obtained, the necessary consent from Ottawa. He will not be allowed to enter Red River as the duly appointed lieutenant-governor."

"We must send a delegation at once to Pembina to determine this," Xavier shouted.

His sentiment was widely and loudly agreed upon by the Mètis. However, the English raised voices of contention.

"We must allow McDougall to enter at once."

Voices in both languages were raised, each side favouring their agenda. Riel stood looking down at the melee, the papers trembling in his hands. Guillaume glanced his way at the moment Riel's features darkened with frustration and temper. He raised his arms and bellowed to quiet the cacophony.

"*Arrêt!* Listen to me!" His face flushed with anger he focused his words on the English Half-Breeds. "Go, return peacefully to your farms. Give this example to your children. But watch us act. We are going ahead to work and obtain a guarantee of our rights and yours. You will come to share them in the end." With a last thunderous glower, he swept out through a back entrance.

Guillaume stared for a moment at the space so recently vacated. The powerful emanations of Riel's presence lingered in the tense atmosphere. He turned to Pierre who was listening to a heated debate between a group of French and English. Guillaume touched his arm and drew him away, toward the rear of the room.

"Louis seems to have put much thought into his List of Rights. I fear McDougall will want no part of it. Equally sure Macdonald in Ottawa won't even read it."

"You don't think they will see how serious we are about protecting our rights?" Pierre objected. "We aren't asking for anything other than our God given right to keep the land we have worked and lived on. Surely, us expecting the right to keep our language and our ability to govern our own community shouldn't be surprising to them."

"We will see, I suppose." Guillaume shrugged. "Do you see Baptiste or Francois anywhere? You know how hot-headed Baptiste can be. I would hate for him to get involved in a brawl with the English. Fighting among ourselves will only serve to make the Canadian position stronger. God knows Mair and Schultz are ever working behind the scenes and with ill intent toward us."

"I don't see either Baptiste or Francois. Let's hope they have left already. We can stop by Baptiste's on the way back to be sure. I agree with you about Schutlz undermining our efforts, I see it everyday while I work when he comes in. He is engaged in some kind of private meetings which he is very careful to keep hidden from me."

"Keep your ears open, *mon ami*. Any information you can acquire may help us. Now, I must find Hugh. I am eager to hear what it is he wants to tell me, and I hope he has the answers to what troubles me."

"Do you want me to stay with you, or leave you to speak with Hugh alone?" Pierre glanced around the room where most of the English had left, muttering, and throwing dark glances at the remaining French.

"This is as much your concern as mine. I know you and Marie-Anne were pledged. She was most fond of you. Come. We will find Hugh together and see what he has to say."

"Louis is a powerful speaker. I hope his leadership will be enough for us to gain and keep the respect and recognition we deserve." Pierre followed his friend toward the door.

"Will!" Hugh O'Lone appeared out of the thinning crowd. "Glad I finally found you in this crush. Now most of the others have left it is easier to see. I don't want to talk here, let's go somewhere more private."

"*Certainement*. Where do you have in mind?"

The three men shouldered their way out of the meeting house into the brisk starlit night. They wended their way past the knots of men gathered along the street. Some discussions were louder than others, under it all ran a thread of unease and the threat of violence.

"We can use the back room at my place. No one will bother us there and the noise of the saloon will cover our words if anyone should be lurking about to listen." O'Lone headed down the dirt street past Schultz's big house toward his brightly lit establishment where music and men spilled out into the street.

Guillaume shouldered his way through the throng of men crowding the saloon. Snatches of conversation told him most of the men were in agreement with the demands of the proposed provisional government, but there was some dissension among them and support for those who favoured the annexation by Upper Canada. Most of the later were the English and Scottish who stood the most to gain if McDougall and the surveyors snatched the land from those already farming it and gave it to the British newcomers.

He followed Hugh into the back room behind Pierre. The closed door shut out the worst of the noise from the front room. He took a chair at the rough table and waited while Hugh poured whisky into three short glasses. The spirit burned down his throat, fumes rising up the back of his nose. It settled into a nice fire in his belly dispelling some of the unease generated by the meeting and the sinking feeling that the Mètis were fighting a losing battle. Guillaume leaned back in his chair, his gaze following the spiral of smoke from Hugh's pipe where it circled the hanging lamp above the table.

"What is it you wish to tell me? Have you heard something that might lead me to the animal who killed my sisters?" He set his whisky glass on the table. "One of the Company men?

"I think you need to look higher than those clerks." Hugh held up a hand as Pierre's expression darkened. "From what I have heard, those two did bother the women that night who were on their way to Schultz's, but the women did make it to their destination. And, those two drink everything they make, unless they stole it, there's no way they would have had any silver button on them. Without a doubt, that button would have been sold or traded for drink. No, I believe you need to look much farther up the pecking order than those."

"We know they were at Schultz's. Do you think they might have seen or heard something that they shouldn't have?" Pierre leaned forward, hands clenched on the edge of the table. "You think it might be Shultz who murdered them?"

O'Lone spread his arms wide, palms of his hands up. "It is possible, but there is nothing linking him to the murder, only that his is the last place they were seen alive. If he thought they might put a wrench in any plans he has that would stop him from turning a tidy profit..."

"They might have accidentally walked in on one of his secret meetings, maybe heard plans those at the meeting didn't want to made public, or were there men there who weren't supposed to be?"

"Plans to support McDougall, maybe smuggle him past the blockade?" Guillaume ground out the words. "The lives of two Mètis women would mean nothing to them, from the comments I have overheard, they would consider it a service to the community."

"I'll kill him with my bare hands." Pierre lurched to his feet, his chair tipping over to crash on the floor. He started for the door.

"Pierre!" Guillaume caught him by the arm. "Hold. We have no proof and if you go after him like this all that will happen is you will end up in jail and if Schultz does have anything to do with their deaths, then we will have alerted him that we suspect him."

"Listen to Will. You must go carefully with this. Shultz has many friends in high places, it would not be beyond his capabilities to plant false evidence and make you out the killer," O'Lone cautioned.

Pierre righted his chair and collapsed into it, elbows on the table and his head resting on his hands. His back tensed as he attempted to control his rapid breathing. Hugh filled his glass with more whisky and pushed it toward Pierre.

Guillaume sat down and reached for his glass, swirling the amber liquid so it caught the light. "I doubt Schultz would do the dirty work himself, he'd get one of his bully boys to do it. Someone might be willing to talk, given the right incentive..." He downed the remaining whisky and got to his feet. "*Merci*, Hugh. You have been most helpful. If you should hear anything else I would appreciate hearing it, *s'il vous plais*. Our conversation has given me much to think about. I believe I will also speak with Riel about these secret meetings at the Shultz house. I'm sure he will find the information quite interesting.

Pierre got up and gripped Guillaume's arm. "I just realized something. I overheard him talking to Mair when he thought I couldn't hear their conversation. Something about him hiding or storing a lot of pork at his warehouse and working out a way to blame Grant and Riel for stealing it. God! If Marguerite and Marie-Anne blundered into something like that, it would sure give Shultz and his friends a good reason to shut them up permanently."

"If we find this is true, I will dump Shultz, and whoever I can get my hands on that is involved, dead into the river with the rest of the pig shit." Guillaume glowered at his clenched hands.

"Go carefully, Will. I don't want to see you kicking at the end of a rope." O'Lone cautioned again.

He snorted. "They would never find me. I'll take the boys and disappear into the woods on the north shores of Lake Winnipeg. I am well equipped to survive in the wilderness. But it won't come to that. Never fear." He favoured O'Lone with a feral grin and moved to the door. Pierre joined him and the two men threaded their way through the clots of drinkers and out into the welcome cool of the night.

Chapter Ten

The fire in the hearth burned low, flames guttering in the draft from Guillaume's entry. Archie rubbed his eyes and levered himself out of the chair by the fire. The acrid scent of scorched food emanated from the pot resting in the coals.

The two boys were sound asleep on their pallets. Archie picked up the poker and gingerly dragged the pot out onto the hearthstone. He removed the lid and stirred the contents.

"It might be a bit burnt. I tried to keep it warm, but I think I fell asleep after the boys did," he apologized.

"It is of no matter, I have eaten already." Guillaume took a rag off the mantle, wrapped it around the handle of the pot and placed it by the door. "We'll see if anything is salvageable in the morning. Right now, I need to ask you more questions about the man you saw the night my sisters were murdered. Come, sit." Gesturing to the chairs by the fire, he sat and stretched his long buckskin clad legs toward the warmth.

Archie perched on the other chair; his hands twisted together. "I already told you what I remember. You ain't gonna throw me out if I can't remember anything else, are you?"

"Non, of course not. As long as you are staying out of trouble and pulling your weight, I have no issue with you staying here." He paused and stared into the flames before adding a bit of fuel. "Take your time, then tell me again everything you remember about that night. Maybe you've forgotten something small that might prove to be very important."

Archie swallowed with an audible gulp, face screwed up with worry and concentration. Guillaume waited, then listened to the boy recite the same information he'd given earlier. Archie's voice trailed off into silence as he finished.

"Honest, I don't remember nothin' else."

"You said you heard this man mutter something, what did his voice sound like? Young, old? His accent, manner of speaking? You told me he smelled clean, what did you mean by that?" Guillaume leaned forward, Hugh's advice forefront in his mind. If the person smelled clean and Archie remembered correctly, the murderer couldn't be one of the trappers or others who had no means of bathing in the cold months. *That would fit with Hugh's thought that the person might be a member of what could be considered the upper class of the area. Doesn't rule out all of the Company men, but perhaps I should be taking a closer look at*

Schultz and his friends, or even Ashmore himself." Guillaume shook his head. Over the months that Marguerite had lived with Ashmore, Guillaume had come to know the man fairly well. His gut said the man wouldn't hurt her, but he wasn't ready to rule anybody out just yet. Archie cleared his throat, breaking into Guillaume's thoughts.

"I said, I think he, the man I mean, had an English accent. Not like mine, more posh, snooty, and kinda high-pitched."

"Are you sure about that?" Guillaume narrowed his eyes, gauging whether the boy was making it up to help ensure he wouldn't be turned out.

"I think so. I never thought it was important before, like. But, yeah, I'm fair sure he was English, not like the strange way those Scotsmen babble on. I cain't never make heads or tails out of half what they say."

"Good, good. Anything else, no matter how small. Think carefully, *fils.*"

Archie closed his eyes and frowned. "He was wearing boots."

"As does just about everyone." Guillaume snorted.

His eyes popped open. "No, no. I mean they were fancy boots. Tall and shiny. I remember they shone in the bit of light there was. I maybe wouldn't have seen that, but I was all crouched down and when he went by me his legs were right in front of my eyes.

And a kinda long coat, it brushed the top of those boots."

"What colour is the coat?" Guillaume prompted. Red, along with the silver button might point to someone with connections to the British military. There were a few of them lurking waiting for McDougall perhaps.

"Dark colour. Blue, I think. Might have been a dark brown, but it wasn't buckskin or fur. Sounded like cloth when it rubbed on the boots. Honest, I was so scairt I could hardly breathe, heart was pounding in me head so loud I worried that bloke would hear it. Near passed out holding me breath too when he went by so close. The angels me Ma used to prat on about must'a been lookin' out fer me."

"You sure it wasn't red? The coat?" Guillaume pressed.

"Could'a bin, I s'pose. It was that dark. But I don't think it was red."

"Did you see anything else. On the boots, like spurs? On the coat or his trousers?"

Archie closed his eyes again while Guillaume bridled his impatience.

"Buttons, on the sleeve near me. Shiny ones. Two or three in a row up the cuff."

Guillaume drew the button found on his sister out of his pouch and gave it to Archie. "Did it look anything like this?"

The boy turned it over in his fingers, held it closer to the fire. "Didn't get a real good look, ye know? Just saw something on the sleeve shine as his arm moved, the buttons might have been silver like this, or maybe gold coloured like brass. Honest, Guillaume, I was scairt half to death and because he was so close, I remembered me Pa telt me to close me eyes if I were hidin' so the shine in the dark wouldn't give me away." He sat up and looked straight at Guillaume. With an absent gesture he handed the button back. "He smelled like lavender. It made me think of me Ma, she would sometimes go away to work in Kent at the lavender fields, and when she come home, she smelled like that. Don't know why I never remembered about that 'til now." The boy shook his head and turned his face toward the fire. "Miss me ma, I do."

"As do I. And my sisters." He leaned over and squeezed Archie's shoulder. "You've been a big help tonight. My thanks for the information and for watching the boys. When did Fèlicitè leave?"

"Not too long before you got home. She had to go help her ma and I told her I'd be fine lookin' after the young'uns."

"Good man." Guillaume gave his shoulder another quick squeeze before sitting back. "Off to bed with you. The sun comes early, and we have much to do, as always."

Archie got to his feet, both hands scrubbing his hair. "Fèlicitè says I must wash tomorrow, especially me hair. Says I stink." He grinned. "She also said to tell you she likes looking after the young'uns and she'll be by tomorrow." Archie sniffed at his shirt and wrinkled his nose. "Guess I do stink, at that. Never noticed until she said. Night"

The rustle of clothing and the sound of water hitting the chamber pot after the boy moved out of the ring of fire light told Guillaume Archie was taking care of the necessary before retiring. He stayed by the fire after banking the coals for the night, pondering the new information Archie just supplied. Hugh's idea of looking higher than the trappers and Company men had merit given what Archie remembered. Fancy boots and shiny buttons on the sleeve of a coat certainly pointed that way, not to mention smelling of lavender. Perhaps he'd just happen to go by Schultz's establishment tomorrow and drop by the Nor'Wester, check out what he might find there. Pierre would be in a good position to take a peek at Schultz's coats, see what colour they were, if they were missing any buttons. Guillaume's fingers played with the button he'd returned to its pouch when Archie gave it back to him earlier. Might also be a good time to see if he could find out what Schultz and his gang were up to. See if there was anything Grant and Riel should be aware of.

* * *

Early the next morning, Guillaume sauntered into the Nor'Wester's offices. The rhythmic crash and bang of the printing

161

press led him to the back room where Pierre was busy at work. He let the press clatter to a halt when Guillaume stepped into his line of sight. Wiping his face with his sleeve, he moved away from the press toward the trays of lead type. In spite of the cold wind blowing outside, it was hot in the small room.

"Where's Shultz?" Guillaume glanced into the small cubby Schultz used as a private office, finding it empty.

"Lit out of here a while ago. Headed to the drug store near as I can figure. What brings you here on such a cold morning?"

"New information from Archie. The person he saw right after the murder smelled like lavender and the coat was dark blue, he thinks, with silver buttons."

"Huh. That explains the button in Marguerite's hand, then doesn't it? And lavender? Puts a new light on things, I'd say. Only one of the toffs would smell like lavender. Only ones who could afford it."

"Hugh thinks the same thing. Not about the lavender, I haven't spoken to him about that. If you recall when we met with him last night he told me I should be looking a little higher than the trappers and Company clerks. I have to think he's right about that."

A group of men passed by the office, hurrying more than the temperature warranted.

"Wonder where they're goin' in such a hurry?" Pierre glanced out the window.

Guillaume shrugged. "How long do you think he will be gone? I wouldn't mind having a look in his office."

"What for?" Pierre frowned.

"What colour coat does he wear?" Guillaume avoided a direct answer. Schultz, along with Mair, was a bastard and openly opposed to the French Half-breeds. Removing two Mètis women who might have come across information they shouldn't have wouldn't trouble his soul at all. Didn't that Anglican Reverend Corbett preach that all half-breeds are miserable savages. And Catholics are all moral degenerates out to conquer the world? The man is like a rabid dog."

Pierre turned back toward his friend. "I don't know how long Schultz be gone but have a look if you like. I'll let you know if I see him coming. Although, I think it's a waste of time. Mair is more likely to smell of whisky or rum than lavender."

Guillaume snorted in agreement and slipped into the tiny office. No sooner had he opened the bottom drawer of the desk than a waft of cold air swirled by him as the outside door swung open. *Merde! Where is Pierre? If that's Schultz...* He scanned the space looking for an escape route. No windows, no place to hide...

"Lord Ashmore, how can I help you?" Pierre's arm snaked into the office and pulled the door shut, closing Guillaume into the room.

Guillaume pressed his ear to the door. Ashmore was a definite sore spot after his cavalier treatment of his children with Marguerite. The two men must have moved away from the office. All he could make out was the rumble of voices but couldn't make out any words. Floorboards creaked as boots clumped toward the door, moments later Pierre opened the door. Guillaume moved into the outer office and sneezed. *Lavender.* His eyes met Pierre's.

"Ashmore! He stinks of lavender, Guillaume ground the words out between clenched teeth.

"Thought I was gonna choke on it," Pierre agreed. "You couldn't see it, but his coat was a dark blue with silver buttons."

"Any of them missing?" Guillaume's eyes narrowed.

"Not that I could see, but I obviously couldn't inspect his clothing, could I?"

"*Non, non.*" Guillaume shook his head. "This complicates matters somewhat, but if I can find proof that he was involved in hurting my sisters he will pay."

"Did you know O'Lone hired that Orangeman Thomas Scott as a bartender?" Pierre changed the subject, hoping to cool his friend's temper.

"Why would he do that?"

"Keep an eye on him? Try to stop him from ranting on about 'depraved half-breeds being the scourge of the earth'? I don't know.

I did hear that the idiot accosted Riel in Winnipeg the other day."

"I can't imagine that went well." Guillaume crooked an eyebrow.

Pierre sighed. "You know Louis, he remained civil and avoided a physical altercation even though Scott was looking for a fight. I think he wanted to provoke Louis into a fight and then claim that he was attacked. Get Riel thrown in jail."

"That sounds like him. Perhaps Shultz put him up to it?"

"Maybe. I haven't heard anything to support that, but Mair has been going to secret meetings at Schultz's place over the store. I heard Schultz wants to raise the Canadian flag on that pole of his to welcome McDougall who is still stuck in Saint Cloud."

"Surely, he's not that foolish? It would cause a riot." Guillaume frowned.

"I think he would welcome that. It would give him an excuse to set up that police force McDougall is sending those rifles for."

"*Oui*, we must go carefully and avoid violence if we can, just as Riel is preaching," Guillaume agreed.

Pierre grinned. "Did you hear about a bunch of us parading past the flagpole the other day singing Falcon's anthem?"

"You mean that song he wrote after the Battle of Seven Oaks?" A smile spread across Guillaume's face.

"That same." Pierre hooked his thumbs in his waistband, threw his head back and began to sing.

> *"Ah would you have seen those Englishmen*
> *And the Bois brûlés a' chasing them,*
> *One by one we did them destroy*
> *While our Bois brûlés uttered shouts of joy"*

"I'm sure he appreciated that."

"Oh, very much."

The two men broke into laughter, leaning on the counter.

"Don't you have work to do?" William Coldwell, Schutlz's erstwhile partner, stood in the doorway, brows drawn together in scowl. He stalked past them, banging his shoulder into Guillaume before disappearing into his office. "Get to work, those pamphlets won't print themselves," he growled, sticking his head out before closing his door.

"Come by the cabin later," Guillaume said as he left.

Pierre nodded, the clang of the printing press following Guillaume out the door. His steps took him down King Street toward the corner where Schutlz's buildings were. He paused at the corner looking past the flagpole to the unfinished brick house. He watched the front of the drug store for a few minutes, nothing out of the ordinary seemed to be happening at the moment. *I wonder what he has hidden in that warehouse of his?* There had been unsubstantiated rumours of those 350 Enfield rifles having been smuggled into the Village of Winnipeg and gossip said Schultz was storing them. Guillaume doubted the accuracy of those tales. There was no way the rifles could have gotten by the blockade on the Fort Garry trail at the Riviere Salè. But what else might he be hiding? Pulling his collar up further on his neck and making sure his knife was snugged in the embroidered red sash at his waist, Guillaume moved down the side street and entered the drug store.

"Mousseau," Schultz acknowledged his presence before pointedly turning to the two Englishmen by the counter.

Guillaume nodded and moved casually around the storefront. He worked his way toward the counter, alert to every move Schultz and his customers made. He waited until the two men left before approaching the counter and purchasing some mint and willow bark. There was no scent of lavender about Schultz, rather he fairly stank of tobacco and smoke. Dropping the payment on the counter, Guillaume left the store. He glanced at the sun, a gleam of silver through the gathering clouds. Time to get home and check on the boys. There was firewood to gather and cut, along with a million other chores that needed seeing to. He needed to make more bannock and pretty soon he'd need to go hunting, the meat supply was getting low. Tucking his head down against the wind blowing up the river, he hurried toward his cabin, hoping Archie had kept the fire going and the two younger boys hadn't given him too hard a time. His thoughts turned to Miles Ashmore. From what he knew of the man, he didn't think he would kill Marguerite in cold blood, strike her down in the dark on the street. But then, how well did he know the Englishman? Not as well as he had thought, it seemed. He needed to pay Ashmore a visit at his home, a chance to get inside and take note of how the man responded when Guillaume brought up the subject of Marguerite's death. It was almost December and Christmas was fast approaching amid all the drama playing out between the Canada Trust Party headed by Charles Mair and the Council of Assiniboia who were appointed by the Hudson Bay governor was coming to a head. That should give him an excuse to ask Ashmore for a meeting, to discuss whether he would provide for his sons at Christmas. Guillaume doubted the English wife would be too receptive to the idea. He grinned.

* * *

The first of December. As good a day as any to visit Ashmore. Guillaume stood on the porch, took a bracing breath, and rapped on the door. He waited; shoulders hunched against the winter air. Losing patience, he knocked hard enough to sting his knuckles. The lace curtain of window beside the door twitched, but no one answered his knock. Cursing, he hammered on the solid door, rattling the glass in the windows on either side. A high feminine voice demanding someone answer the door preceded the click of boot heels on polished wood. The door opened a crack.

"Good afternoon. Please tell Lord Ashmore that Guillaume Mousseau wishes to speak with him." Guillaume prudently stuck a foot over the threshold to prevent the servant from shutting the door.

The thin pale face blanched paper-white and the eyes widened in the drawn face. Thin lips parted but no sound emerged.

"If you please, I wish to speak with His Lordship," Guillaume insisted.

The door opened further, the servant glanced over his shoulder in response to firm steps approaching from deeper within the house. Guillaume took the opportunity to step into the front hall. The door swung shut behind him. A blonde woman, dressed in what Guillaume assumed was the latest fashion in London, swept toward him. He had to admit she was beautiful and much younger than her husband. He took in the determined set of her chin and the imperious expression in her eyes and realized that Ashmore must have his hands full with this woman.

"What is it you want? You most certainly do not have an invitation to invade my home." Charlotte Ashmore regarded him as she might a bug on her carpet. Even though she had to tilt her head back to glare into his face, the woman gave the distinct impression she was indeed staring down her nose at him.

"I wish to speak with your husband." Guillaume tipped his head in a small bow.

"What is it you wish to speak with him about? My husband is a very busy man," Charlotte's tone was chill, the words clipped.

"The matter is between Ashmore and myself." He returned her cold stare.

"What concerns my husband also concerns me." She turned to the servant who seemed to be trying to merge into the wallpaper. "You may leave us, Gregory."

The man threw Guillaume a look like a hunted fox and scurried down the hall to disappear into the bowels of the building. *Odd little man.* Guillaume's nose twitched when Charlotte took a step neared, the scent of lavender rising from the rustle of her skirts. He resisted the urge to rub his nose.

"Now, let us speak clearly. My husband is not at home, and even if he were, I would not allow *you* into my home. It would please me if you left now." She gestured toward the door.

"I wish to speak with your husband about his sons and how he plans to provide for them in the coming holidays." Guillaume shut his eyes for a moment and repressed the urge to turn this presumptuous *fille* over his knee and smack some respect into her. Opening them, he found her glaring at him, foot tapping the polished floor.

"My husband has no sons. I am his lawful wife and we have not yet been blessed with children. Now get out!" She fired the last words at him, eyes blazing.

"I must disagree, *madame*. I assure you his sons are alive and well and they ask for their father often."

"I repeat, my husband has no sons. Those creatures you refer to are abominations. Reverend Corbett denounces the offspring of your kind, and indeed all Catholics as moral degenerates. Please, do remove yourself from my presence or shall I have you removed?"

Realizing he was getting nowhere with this woman and finding himself increasingly sickened by her bigotry, Guillaume turned to the door. "I will seek Ashmore elsewhere. Good day, *madame*." He reached for the handle, his arm brushing against a blue coat hanging on the hall tree by the door. His sharp eyes noticed a button missing on the sleeve. A silver button. He spun back toward the woman so swiftly she took a step backward hand, pressed to her throat. She snatched a bell sitting on a spindly table set against the wall and rang it loudly.

"Whose coat is this?" Guillaume shook the coat sleeve at her.

Her eyes widened and she shook the bell harder. "That is none of your business."

"Is it Ashmore's" He dropped the sleeve and took a step toward her.

Running feet echoed from deep in the house and three large men burst down the hall, one of them armed with a pitchfork. Charlotte ceased ringing her bell and stepped to the side. "Remove this person from my house," she commanded. Her gaze swept over him, and she gave a dismissive sniff of her aristocratic nose.

"I will have the answers I seek," he assured her, before reaching behind him to open the door. He backed out of the opening, not trusting the angry men not to hit him from behind. Guillaume stepped out of the suffocating warmth of Ashmore's house and took a deep breath of cold air. It helped to ease his temper, but he couldn't get the image of the coat sleeve with its missing silver button. The coat in question wasn't blue though, it was a dark green. Perhaps Archie was mistaken about the colour of the coat he saw, or perhaps... He shook his head and turned his steps toward Pierre's cabin. He would search out Ashmore later, convince him to provide Christmas gifts for his sons, as he'd done in the past. Failing that, Guillaume would make sure the boys and Archie enjoyed the celebration of the birth of Christ. His thoughts touched on the Anglican Reverend Corbett. How could a man of God preach such malicious things about others who worshipped the same God? The pettiness and bigotry of some was tearing the community apart and pitting Protestants against Catholics and relegating the indigenous segment of the population into obscurity. Nothing good could come out of such a situation.

Chapter Eleven

Guillaume joined the gathering of men near Schultz's establishment on December 1, 1869. The men milled around, throwing glares toward the warehouse where wagons loaded with pork that was supposed to feed the surveyors and road construction crews of the Canadian government waited.

"What is Schutlz up to now?" Baptiste tucked his gun under his arm and adjusted his scarf against the cold.

"Stealing is what. He's planning to send that pork on to Portage la Prairie to the Loyalists there. Riel says we need to stop them because the rumours say Schultz is planning to place the blame for the missing pork on us," Pierre said.

"Do we know this for certain?" Guillaume wanted to avoid distractions from hunting for his sisters' murderer, but if the rumours were true….his place was here.

Baptiste spat on the ground and glared at the wagons. "*Oui*. The man sought out Louis and offered to pay him whatever he wanted to keep his mouth shut and say nothing. Of course, Louis refused. And this is why he has called us here."

"Is there no end to what these members of the Canadian Party will stoop too?" Guillaume growled.

Baptiste shrugged. "This may be just Schutlz trying to put some money in his own pocket. So now we will guard both the home and the business day and night. We are to harm no one, but we will not allow those wagons to move."

"How many of us are there?" Pierre surveyed the mass of Mètis and supporters.

"I'm not sure of the exact number. So we wait and see what happens." Baptiste hunched deeper into his coat.

* * *

Guillaume shifted on the log stump, one of many ringing the large fire, laughing, and jesting with the men he'd just beaten in a foot race. While he agreed with Riel that the pork needed to be guarded, it was mind numbingly boring. Guillaume was aching for something to happen. The foot races helped to pass the time and keep the men moving, but they wore thin after a while. The rest of the time, mostly during the long dark hours of the early December nights, were spent exchanging tales with each other. Some of them wildly exaggerated, some only mildly. The Mètis were in possession of Fort Garry, and he hoped that would continue. There were rumours flying that Colonel Dennis was planning to attack Fort Garry and the

Canadian's hope was he would liberate the fort and Winnipeg. Placing it back in the Canadian's hands. He rose to greet the men arriving to relieve the men currently guarding, greeting them, and exchanging what little information there was on the situation within the house. Shouldering his rifle, he walked with Pierre to O'Lone's for a drink before heading home.

* * *

A few days later, Riel appeared before a gathering of men, Guillaume among them. A paper fluttered in his hand. The wind was bitter and it was hard to hear what was being said. The word passed through the men. Colonel Dennis had been appointed 'Conservator of Peace' by McDougall after McDougall had sent a document with Colonel Dennis to Schultz at the Nor'Wester proclaiming himself, by order of the queen, the lieutenant governor of both the Northwest and Rupert's Land that were now part of Canada. The paper Riel held in his hand was Dennis' commission commanding his soldiers to attack, arrest, disarm and disperse the Mètis and then to burn their homes and businesses. After reading it, Riel tore the paper in pieces and threw them into the snow at his feet. A roar of anger surged through the crowd.

176

"Is it true, that this McDougall now thinks he rules over us?" Guillaume shook his head.

"It is true," Pierre said. "I was at the Nor'Wester office when that *saloud* Dennis showed up. He had a royal proclamation declaring McDougall Lieutenant Governor and giving him power over us. Even though he is still being held back in Pembina. Schultz printed the copies himself and then distributed them all over the village. I see he has them plastered all over his front door."

"Riel needs to shut that paper down. And quickly," Guillaume ground out the words. "Everything he prints is full of lies and half-truths. All intended to support his cause and destroy the rest of us."

"I think about quitting at least four times a day, but Louis asks me to stay on so I can pass on any information that may benefit our cause or alert us to what we must watch out for." Pierre frowned and wrapped his scarf tighter around his neck. "Dennis has disappeared after dropping off that proclamation. I hear he is off trying to muster up men in order to attack the Stone Fort. It seems he thinks we hold that rather than Fort Garry."

"Good luck to him then." Guillaume laughed and clapped his friend on the back.

* * *

Guillaume rolled out of bed on December 4, grabbing his rifle as he came to his feet. The door of the cabin rattled with the blows. Shaking the sleep from his brain, he recognized Baptiste's voice and set the rifle down. "It's okay. Go back to sleep. It's only Baptiste. I will take care of things," he assured his alarmed nephews. He glanced at Archie and motioned him to roll out of his blankets and pick up the rifle. Just in case... Archie complied positioned himself to the side of the door, rifle cocked and ready.

"*À venir*, Baptiste. What is wrong?" He nodded at Archie before removing the bar from the door and pulling it open. His friend shoved into the room followed by Fèlicitè. Archie uncocked the rifle and leaned it beside the door. Fèlicitè moved to soothe the two younger boys who were tangled together, watching with wide frightened eyes. Archie hovered by the two older men, anxious to hear what had them so excited.

"Schultz. Louis has sent out a call for more men. Hurry," Baptiste vibrated with supressed energy.

"What has happened?" Guillaume shrugged into his outer clothes and grabbed his rifle. "You stay here," he ordered Archie who was already dressed and by the door.

"I want to go. I'm big enough to help." Archie met the older man's gaze, his jaw clenched. "I want to help."

"You are too young yet, *mon chère*." Fèlicitè crossed the room to put an arm around his thin shoulders. "I need you here to help me keep these two in order."

"I can help," Archie insisted but let the young woman herd him toward the fire.

"Come, I will make breakfast for you three boys." Fèlicitè set about stirring the porridge in the pot sitting in the coals.

"Behave yourselves." Guillaume spoke to all three boys but centred his stern gaze on Archie. "I need you to stay here and guard Fèlicitè and the boys."

Archie nodded and went to gather up the clay plates and mugs from the cupboard in the corner.

"Bar the door behind me," Guillaume said, stepping out of the cabin with Baptiste.

They joined a steady flow of other men headed into the village. From the snatches of sentences Guillaume caught as they moved, it seemed something was happening at Schultz's. "Are they trying to move the government pork again?"

"I don't know. I only know Louis has called for another hundred men to attend him."

When they arrived at the warehouse, nothing seemed different than when he left it the night before. The doors and windows were still barricaded. Guillaume and Baptiste pushed through the throng until they found Pierre and some others they knew. O'Lone stood by Guillaume's shoulder.

A flurry of movement at the house brought all the gathered men to attention. Schultz and company were engaged in loading what appeared to be household goods into the wagons now emptied of the contentious pork which was safely back in the warehouse. The men shifted uneasily. Someone ran off to advise Riel and his committee of the situation. The wagons loaded; the situation was a stand-off.

Before too long, a group of sympathizers arrived, some forty-five of them with their wives and children. They all crammed into Schutlz's house, where word came down that some four hundred rounds of ammunition were being distributed to the men inside. Guillaume watched as all the doors and windows were barricaded in quick order. While his pulse quickened at the prospect of action, another part of him wished it was over and done with. His loyalties were solidly with his Mètis brothers, but the unsolved murders of his sisters rested heavy on his heart.

At least Riel had finally shut down the Nor'Wester and James Ross's Red River Pioneer. Both papers spreading anti-Mètis and anti-Catholic sentiment.

* * *

For two days nothing much happened. The Mètis stayed on high alert while rumours of a plan to assassinate Riel ran rampant through the community. The supposed assassins were Thomas Scott, the contentious Orangeman and Alexander McArthur. Since both men were thought to be barricaded in the house with the rest of the sympathizers, Guillaume wondered how the pair were planning to fulfill that quest. It was more likely just a rumour to cover up some other plot. But what that plot could be was a mystery and it worried him.

"Guns! In the windows!"

The cry passed quickly through the crowd. All mirth disappeared from the men gathered outside and guns were trained on the buildings. The two cannons were ordered to be wheeled up from Fort Garry to bolster their defense. For a while it appeared that nothing was going to come of the show of force from within the house.

"Two men, escaping!" The cries came from the guards at the rear of the house.

Guillaume and Pierre, along with Baptiste rushed to add their numbers to the few men posted behind the house and warehouse. Guillaume plunged through the men chasing the two escapees, rifle slung over his back. He caught sight of the back on one man splitting off and ducking between two shacks. Slipping on the snowy ground, Guillaume changed course and followed. The tall thin figure glanced back over his shoulder and redoubled his efforts. Where he thought he was going to run to was a mystery to Guillaume, but he lengthened his stride and gained ground. The man made another quick change of direction, leaping across a ditch and headed for the river.

"I think not, *mon ami*," Guillaume hissed between his teeth. There must be a boat of some kind waiting on the Red River for the two men. His foot slid again on the frozen ground. He was close enough now to hear the gasping of the man's breath. Still running easily, Guillaume closed the distance.

The tall man glanced over his shoulder once more and in turning back lost his footing on a patch of slick ice and went down hard on his side. Guillaume wasted no time in pinning the man and tying his hands with a rawhide thong before dragging him to his feet. It was one of the supposed assassins. Thomas Scott. One hand firmly grasping the man's collar, Guillaume marched him back toward the main body of men still guarding the house and warehouse.

"Hah, you caught him, Will." O'Lone clapped Guillaume on the back. "They have the other man over there." He pointed toward a cluster of men surrounding Riel.

Guillaume shoved Scott toward them, unable to see who the other captive was. The crowd divided, allowing the two men to reach the front. Scott stumbled to a halt beside his co-escapee. Guillaume recognized Alexander McArthur, another Orange sympathizer and stalwart supporter of

Schultz and the Canada Party along with their imperialistic beliefs.

Riel ordered both men be marched to Fort Garry and placed in the prison cells there to await further developments. The big bear-like man seemed undisturbed about the fact these were the two men whose names had been rumoured about as his assassins.

"That was mad, Guillaume. I never knew you could run that fast." Archie looked up at him, face glowing.

"What the devil are you doing here?" Guillaume blustered. "I told you to stay at the cabin with the boys."

Archie hung his head for a moment, then straightened his shoulders. "I'm a good shot, and I'm old enough to fight too. You can't make me stay home."

Guillaume sighed. "Does Fèlicitè know where you are?"

"I told her, she tried to stop me, but I snuck out when she was tending Ètienne." Archie's eyes widened; his gaze fixed on something through the crowd. "That's him!" The words squeaked out and he pointed down the street, starting to shove through the men around him.

"Arret! Where are you going?" Guillaume caught Archie by the collar and hauled him back.

"That man! I saw him, that's the man!" The boy struggled to get free.

"What man?" Guillaume leaned down to stare into his face.

"The man! You know, the man. From that...that...night," Guillaume stuttered.

"The one you saw when you were hiding?" Guillaume straightened up and raked the crowd with his gaze.

"Where? Where did you see him?" He lifted Archie and set him on his shoulder so the boy could see over the crowd.

"I don't see him now, but he went between those buildings, like he was heading toward the river."

"What was he wearing? That same coat?" Guillaume signalled to Pierre who fell into step beside them.

Archie shook his head. "Yes, I recognize the coat. I know it was him. Something about the way he walked and just sort of slid through the crowd. Like he didn't want to be noticed.'

Guillaume set the boy down and lengthened his stride. Archie trotted to keep up to the older men. They turned the corner at the end of the street and paused. Guillaume looked both ways, nothing on the road toward Fort Garry. The road ran along the river, curving toward James Ross' house."

"There! There! See him...Oh, he's gone..." Archie pointed toward Fire Engine Street where the Ashmore residence sat on the corner, just at the start of the curve.

"Are you sure?" Guillaume gripped the boy the shoulders.

Archie nodded so hard his hair fell across his face shaken loose from the wool hat he had crammed on it.

"Ashmore," Pierre hissed the name.

"You're sure you saw the man we are seeking go into the house. That house." Guillaume gestured with his chin toward Ashmore's house.

"Not the house, but into the yard, yes." Archie confirmed.

Guillaume released the boy and moved to catch up with Pierre who was already striding toward the corner. He fell into step beside his friend leaving Archie to trot behind them. "We must be careful, Pierre. We can't just accuse Ashmore or his servant, or he'll have us up before the Council," Guillaume warned. His temper was up as well, but he had no desire to give Ashmore any opening to turn the tables on them.

"Careful, be damned. I will wring the scoundrel's neck with my bare hands." Pierre quickened his pace.

"Wait." He pulled Pierre to the side of the road. "Let me go ahead and speak with the man. You and Archie stay out of sight but where you can see the door. If Archie says Ashmore is the man we seek, then we will make a plan. Since McDougall made his damned proclamation the Council of Assiniboia no longer has any power. The Company has sold Rupert's Land and us to Canada."

"But as we hold Fort Garry and the rolls of land ownership, perhaps Riel will soon declare his provisional government as the rule of law," Pierre said, the angry red fading from his cheeks, the heaving of the great chest slowing.

"Pray God that happens soon. Now, find your place and I will go see if Ashmore will come to the door."

Guillaume waited until the pair were in place before striding up to the door. He hammered on the wood with his fist, unmindful of any vestige of politeness. Ashmore, himself opened the door.

"What is the meaning of this intrusion?" He glowered at the buckskin clad man on his doorstep.

"Where were you this morning?" Guillaume put a booted foot on the threshold to stop any attempt to shut the door.

"That is none of your business." Ashmore started to withdraw and made to close the door.

Guillaume placed a large hand flat on the wood and shoved. Ashmore was forced back a step. "I asked where you were this morning. I'm sure you've heard of the excitement at Schutlz's earlier."

"As I said before, my whereabouts are none of your business. However, if it will get you off my doorstep, I will tell you I was here taking care of some paperwork." One hand smoothed the sleeve of his blue jacket. A sleeve that had all its silver buttons in place.

"Was there anything else?" Ashmore looked pointedly at the dirty boot blocking his doorway.

"What do you plan to do about Christmas gifts for your sons? They are expecting something from their father as you gave them gifts last year and the years before." Guillaume sought to buy time with the request while surreptitiously glancing over Ashmore's shoulder. If it wasn't Ashmore they had seen ducking into the house, then who was it? One of the servants? But which one?

Ashmore glanced over his shoulder, no doubt making sure his wife wasn't in hearing distance. Guillaume let the thought dance through his mind, his eyes darting toward the oak hallstand beside the door that held outerwear.

"I will arrange something for the boys. Now, are we finished here?"

"I suppose I will have to take your word about the paperwork. I will be back if those gifts do not appear," he warned, removing his foot from the doorway.

"I suppose you will." Ashmore closed the door.

Guillaume caught a glimpse of someone entering the hall from the far end, along with a snatch of conversation.

"I have the news you requested, sir. And the items Lady. Ashmore requested..." a man's voice echoed dimly as the door shut.

"Hah! Someone did just return from town," Guillaume whispered as he left the doorway and turned toward where Pierre and Archie waited.

"It wasn't that man," Archie said. "Too tall."

"I'm not surprised. As the door was closing, I heard another man, a servant, who I think just came back from the shops. It must have been him we saw. The man you say you saw the night my sisters were murdered."

"Who was it?" Pierre gripped his arm.

Guillaume shook his head. "I didn't see the man, only heard him. I wonder how many servants the Ashmore's have. At least two that I've seen, a couple of house maids."

"I'll run along to the saloons and see what I can find out. You know how men talk when they're drinking and there must be some who have made deliveries or who worked on the changes that young wife of his insisted on." Pierre snugged his hat down over his ears. "It seemed like things were well in hand at Schultz's and our shift is over."

Guillaume clapped him on the shoulder. "Come by the cabin later if you have time. Any news you might find will be welcome. In the meantime," he put a firm hand on Archie's arm, "this one and I must have a conversation about obeying orders. Non?"

"Yes, sir." Archie hunched his shoulders and dropped his gaze.

"Do not be too hard on the boy. If he hadn't been with us, we wouldn't have noticed the man we tracked to Ashmore's." Pierre gave the boy an encouraging grin.

Guillaume shook his head, and with Archie trudging at his side, the pair made their way through the cold and falling snow back to the cabin.

Chapter Twelve

The morning of December 7, 1869, Guillaume joined the mass of men milling in front of Shultz's properties. The two cannons Riel had ordered wheeled up from Fort Garry earlier were positioned pointed toward the house. Guillaume doubted Riel would actually fire on the house knowing the wives and children of the men were also inside. In spite of his fiery nature and impassioned speeches, the man seemed to want to avoid violence at all costs.

Pierre shoved through the crowd and joined him. "Looks like maybe three hundred of us. Those inside must be shitting their pants."

"At least the idiot decided not to run that Canada Party flag up his damned flagpole. I don't think even Louis could have held back the men if they saw that." Guillaume shrugged deeper into his coat.

"How is Archie this fine day?" Pierre asked.

"Fine and well. He understands why he needs to listen and obey what I ask of him." He paused and sighed. "Although, it was a stroke of luck he was with us yesterday and recognized that man in the crowd. I just wish we had a better idea of who he is."

"I hung around Hugh's saloon for a bit yesterday. You know Louis has closed down the Nor'Wester, so I have time on my hands. I got to talking to a trapper whose sister works for Lady. Ashmore, does laundry and other chores the English maid refuses to do."

"Did you get a name?" Guillaume's hands tightened on his rifle.

Pierre shook his head. "No. Josie, that's his sister, rarely gets out of the kitchen area. One of the man servants brings down the night soil for her to clean. There are two man servants, from what I could gather from Xavier. So it must have been one of them we saw yesterday."

"And it must be one of them who murdered Marguerite and Marie-Anne." Guillaume's face was thunderous.

"But why, Guillaume? Why would an English servant go out in the dark and cold to hunt down two innocent women? It makes no sense." Pierre ran a hand over his beard.

"Unless..." Guillaume closed his eyes and frowned. "Unless someone ordered them to do so." He opened his eyes and met Pierre's gaze. "It might not have been Ashmore who Archie saw walking by his hiding place, but whoever it was may very well have been following Ashmore's orders."

"How in the name of heaven are we ever going to prove that? We don't even know which of the servants it was right now, let alone have any evidence to implicate Ashmore or his man. The Company will still protect the English, even in light of that damned proclamation. You know that Louis feels there is something not quite right with that piece of paper?" Pierre stamped his feet in the fur lines boots. "Damn, it's freezing."

"*Oui*, I heard Louis questioning the timing of the proclamation and wondering how it came to be, contrary to what he heard from friends in Quebec who wrote that Macdonald was hesitating in light of our resistance. But again, there is no proof of duplicity, and Colonel Dennis, damn him to hell, delivered the paper to Schultz."

"I wonder what is going on?" Guillaume moved toward a cluster of men around Riel. He shouldered his way to the front, finding a place next to Riel and listened without adding to the conversation. Riel wanted to negotiate with the men holed up inside the house. Andrew Bannatyne, a Mason who was sympathetic to Riel's cause, shoved his way to Riel's side. Bannatyne was a member of the Council of Assiniboia and in partnership with Alexander Begg, commanded the largest merchant firm in Red River. He argued his position as a friend of both sides, so to speak, that he would be the best man to go in and negotiate a non-violent end to the stand-off. After much debate, Riel agreed and sent Bannatyne in demanding unconditional surrender by the men inside the house.

Schultz refused and insisted on a long list of non-negotiable conditions, without which, he vowed they would not quit the premises. Bannatyne reported on his return, that inside the house they had run out of fresh water, food, and fuel, but Schultz and company refused to budge. After much debate, Riel asked his adjutant general, Ambroise Lèpine to take in the agreement he wrote out on a bit of paper. Lèpine agreed, taking the paper, and tucking it into his belt. Baptiste Morin stepped forward and insisted on accompanying Lèpine, saying that it was irresponsible to send just one of their number in alone. If nothing else, it would give the besieged men a chance to gain a hostage if only one of Riel's men went in. The two men went in and presented the following agreement to the group inside the house.

Dr. Schultz and his men are hereby ordered to give up their arms and surrender themselves. Their lives will be spared should they comply. In case of refusal, all the English Half-breeds and other native women and children are at liberty to depart unmolested.

He told Lèpine and Morin to give the Canadians fifteen minutes to make their decision, sign the document and surrender. Otherwise a full assault on the property would ensue, including the use of the two cannons. Guillaume supressed a shudder and sent a silent prayer winging to the All Mighty that common sense would prevail inside the house and no innocent blood would be shed. From the expression on Riel's face, Guillaume was sure the man was hoping the same, but was committed to ending the stand-off in whatever way possible. Backing down now would put an end to any resistance and chance of the provision government becoming a reality.

The large group of armed French Half-breeds and their supporters shifted uneasily. All eyes focussed on the door of the house, alert to any sounds of gunfire or fighting. Eventually, before the fifteen minutes were up, Lèpine and Morin emerged from the house with the signed document. Guillaume released the breath he hadn't realized he was holding. His gaze met Riel's over the heads of shorter men. A moment of understanding passed between them, Riel crossed himself and glanced skyward before taking possession of the signed agreement. Guillaume turned toward the house where the besieged men were marched out at gunpoint.

Lèpine reported that it was John O'Donnell, the doctor who travelled with McDougall's party who came to his senses first. He told the others they were in an impossible corner and if they didn't surrender there would be massive bloodshed and many innocents, including their wives and children would be caught in the crossfire. O'Donnell stepped forward and was the first to sign.

"Everyone else, including Schultz, came around and signed after that. Except that idiot, Mair. He kept refusing and insisting they all fight to the death. Thank God, the others ignored him and lined up ready to be removed under the supervision of armed French Half-Breeds. Finally, Mair had no other choice than to sign and fall into line."

Guillaume and Pierre, along with Hugh O'Lone, joined the men lining the route to the prison cells at Fort Garry.

"What are those women about?" Pierre frowned at Eliza Mair, Anne Schultz, along with O'Donnell's wife, as they insisted on accompanying their husbands. The rest of the women wisely gathered their children and hurried off toward their homes.

"Oh for the love of God," Guillaume swore and took a step forward before O'Lone stopped him.

"Let Schultz deal with it," Hugh advised. "I doubt he would welcome your assistance."

Anne Schultz crumpled to a heap of skirts on the frozen ground. Her husband picked her up and settled her in a nearby cutter which he preceded to haul by hand, struggling to keep up with the rest of the prisoners.

"Guillaume watched the sorry procession wend its way by his position. The line of prisoners trudged along Main Street between the watchful eyes of Riel's soldiers who held their rifles at ready should any decide to make a run for it. When the last of the group disappeared through the huge gates of Fort Garry Guillaume joined in the celebration, the *feu du joi,* releasing volley after volley of gunfire into the air. His ears ringing as silence prevailed at last, he drew a breath of relief. If the leaders at Fort Schultz, as the premises had taken to be called by the French Half-breeds during the stand-off, hadn't surrendered he feared that even Riel's deep aversion to violence couldn't have stemmed the flow of blood.

"Come, let us go home." Guillaume shouldered his rifle and fell into step beside Pierre as they turned toward their cabins. "I am sure Fèlicitè and the boys will have heard the commotion and not know what to make of it."

Pierre remained silent, a thoughtful expression on his face, while their fur lined foot ware made little sound on the frozen road. As if coming to some inner decision, he cleared his throat and addressed his friend. "Baptiste's daughter seems to be spending a lot of time at your cabin...do you have any intentions toward her?

"*Quoi*?" Guillaume tripped over his own feet as he swung toward his friend in astonishment. "Why would you think such a thing?"

Pierre hid his amusement and kept striding into the wind coming up the river. "The girl is more than of age for marriage, you need someone to help with the boys now and according to Baptiste she would be more than willing." He threw a sideways glance at the tall, bearded man stomping along at his side.

"That may be," Guillaume spoke slowly, shifting the rifle resting on his shoulder. "I have not given it much thought, other than to be grateful she is willing to lend me a hand."

"Do you not think it might be more than gratitude she might be hoping for?"

Guillaume frowned. "Alex did make some comment about something similar a while ago. I had other things on my mind and haven't thought of it since.

"Perhaps you should give it some serious thought, *mon ami*. I will see you tomorrow" Pierre veered off toward his cabin, leaving Guillaume to carry on toward his own.

* * *

"What happened? Did you win?" Archie threw himself at Guillaume as soon as he stepped through the door. "We heard all the guns going off. Was there a big fight? Are you hurt?"

"I am fine." Guillaume extracted himself from Archie, sharing an amused look with Fèlicitè over his head. He shrugged out of his coat and leaned the rifle by the door.

"Come, sit. I have some stew left over from earlier." Fèlicitè handed him a clay mug of hot liquid.

He settled into the chair by the fire, cradling the warmth in his large hands. The three boys crowded around him eager to hear what caused the noise earlier. Fèlicitè perched on the edge of the other chair, gaze fixed on his face.

"The siege of Fort Schultz is ended, peaceably." He took the horn spoon from his belt and shovelled stew into his mouth.

"What was all the gunfire then?" Alex asked, eyes wide in his thin face.

"Ah. That was the victors celebrating as all the prisoners were escourted into Fort Garry headed for the prison cells."

"Truly? Does this mean our troubles with the Canadians stealing our land is over?" Fèlicitè's brown eyes searched his face.

Guillaume shook his head. "I wish that were so, but I fear Macdonald and his friends in Upper Canada will not be so easily dissuaded from annexing Rupert's Land and the NorthWest."

"Why can't they leave us alone?" she cried, throwing up her hands. "We are doing them no harm."

"They do not care. They see Rupert's Land as the doorway to the west and the few in the upper levels see it as a route to easy money. Just look at how Schultz, and a few others, are taking advantage and buying up script for very little of its worth." Guillaume frowned.

"What will they do with all that land though? Surely, they don't intend to farm it?" She twisted her hands in her apron.

Guillaume snorted with derisive amusement. "Not at all. They will gather and hold as much as they can and then hope to sell it at a huge profit once the Company is thoroughly pushed out and the Canadians are in charge."

"That's not fair!" Fèlicitè's eyes flashed. "They are stealing the land for almost nothing, preying on our people's fears."

"*Oui*, they are doing exactly that. It is my hope that Riel and his proposed provisional government will help protect our interests."

"Tell us what happened at the house," Archie urged him. "Was there fighting?"

"What of the women and children?" Fèlicitè asked.

Guillaume ruffled Archie's hair. "No fighting. Messieurs Lèpine and Morin went in with our demands and we stood firm until they agreed to an unconditional surrender." He glanced toward Fèlicitè. "The women and children were allowed to leave unmolested. However, Madame Schultz and Mair insisted on accompanying their husbands to Fort Garry. Even though Madame Schultz appeared very ill, she collapsed on leaving the house and her husband had to bundle her into a cutter which he was forced to drag by himself. I wonder at her decision." He shook his head.

"Poor woman," Fèlicitè shook her head, "even if she is rude to me and Maman if we pass her on the streets, I will pray she is better soon."

"I have no doubt Riel will see that she receives the care she needs," Guillaume assured her.

"I will pray all the same." She got to her feet. "It is getting late, and I must go help Maman. All is in order here for the night, I think."

Guillaume got to his feet as well. "Oui, of course. You must go at once before it gets full dark. I can go with you, make sure you get home safely."

"The boys..." She glanced at Ètienne curled up now by the fire. Alex playing with some sticks he was fashioning into something."

"Archie can take care of them for the little time it will take for me to see you safely home. After Marguerite and Marie-Anne... Your *père* would never forgive me if something happened to you because of your association with me."

Fèlicitè's argument died in her throat as she took in the grief evident in his expression. "*Mais, oui.* I would appreciate your company." She bundled herself into her shawls and with a last glance at Archie she followed Guillaume out the door. "You don't think the attack was aimed at you? Hurting you by hurting your family?"

""I don't know and therefore I am taking no chances. Baptiste trusts me to be sure you are safe, and I wish you safe for your own self." Guillaume pulled the door shut behind them.

Chapter Thirteen

The next morning found Guillaume making his way to St. Boniface College. Pierre and Baptiste, along with a host of other supporters, moved in an orderly fashion toward their destination.

Baptiste and Fèlicitè arrived earlier at the cabin with news that Louis Riel was preparing to proclaim a provisional government for the Northwest Territories. He was reported to have declared that if the English didn't care to co-operate, the French would proceed alone. Leaving Fèlicitè to mind the boys, Guillaume pulled on his coat and stamped into his boots and left with Baptiste.

"Guillaume!"

A tug on his sleeve and a breathless voice startled him out of his thoughts. Glancing to his left, a knot of anger formed in his chest. "Archie! What the devil are you doing here? Return home at once. This may not be safe, there might be some violence."

The young man fell into step beside him. "I am old enough to take care of myself." His mouth set in a determined line, he marched along, eyes ahead, not meeting Guillaume's gaze. "Fèlicitè says this is a historic moment and I don't want to miss it. She said it is important for our future."

"That may be true, but there is no guarantee there will not be trouble." Guillaume paused and caught Archie's arm. "If I send you back, you will just follow anyway, won't you?"

Archie shrugged and kept walking.

"Ah, let him come along," Baptiste said, throwing an arm around the young man's shoulder. "As he says, he is old enough, and the young should be here to hear and remember Riel's words. It is indeed a moment in our history."

"See that you stay beside me and if trouble arises you will do as I say, *compris*?" Guillaume gave in, knowing Archie would just double back and come along anyway if he insisted on sending him home.

The group of supporters arrived at St. Boniface College and gathered by the steps waiting for Riel to appear.

"Riel has been up all night with Father Dugas and Father Ritchot deciding what principals must be included to ensure the legitimacy and legality of the proposed government. The talk is the document will be called The Declaration of the People of Rupert's Land." Hugh O'Lone joined them. "I was just talking to one of the men who has been supplying refreshments for the men who are holed up in a small room inside the college."

"How are they planning to accomplish this?" Pierre shuffled his feet in the cold.

"Riel has been influenced by the English philosopher Thomas Hobbes. Here," he pulled a crumpled sheet of paper out of his pocket, "this was given to me by the same man who took in food and drink. It came from the trash, but he said it gives the general idea of what they are planning."

Guillaume took the paper, shielding it from the wind. Pierre and Baptiste leaned in to read it as well while Archie hovered anxious to hear what was written.

Guillaume muttered the words out loud. "Where, it is admitted by all men as a fundamental principle that the public authority commands the obedience and respect of its subjects. It is also admitted that a people, when it has no government, is free to adopt one form of government in preference to another to give or to refuse allegiance to that which is proposed." He turned the paper over to squint at the blotched ink and crossed out words. "Riel says here in the scribbles that since the Hudson's Bay Company has abandoned Rupert's Land without consulting with the inhabitants so that dissolves the obligation of those people to be loyal to the HBC or to any imposed Successor. Since, he argues, there is no legitimate government in place, the Mètis are free to choose a government of their own." Guillaume shook his head.

"I can't imagine McDougall or Macdonald will be too pleased with such a declaration," Hugh observed.

"Perhaps, they will have nothing to say in the matter. In any case, I stand in support of Riel," Guillaume said, handing the much distressed paper back to Hugh.

"And I," declared Pierre and Baptiste.

"Me, also," Archie chimed in.

"Look! Here is Riel now." Hugh pointed toward the doors of the college.

The gathered men surged forward in an effort to hear what was being said. Riel announced that John Bruce would head the provisional government, and Louis himself would be the secretary. He insisted the Mètis remember they were still loyal to the British crown but through the creation and declaration of this provisional government they would now have the right to negotiate the terms on which Canadian authority could be established in the Northwest.

A rousing cheer rose from the men. Guillaume noted that although Bruce was the appointed president it was Riel who spoke to the gathering in his compelling and eloquent way. His passion for the cause and his charisma swept the men up and carried them along in his enthusiasm. Riel implored the assembled men to be sure to attend mass on Friday December 10, 1869, then he and Bruce disappeared back into the college. A few men passed out printed papers bearing the Proclamation of the Provisional

Government. Guillaume grasped one as a sheaf of papers passed by him.

Hunkering down with Pierre and O'Lone, he read the document, nodding in approval.

Proclamation by the Provisional Government, Dec. 8, 1869.

Whereas, it is admitted by all men, as a fundamental principle, that the public authority commands the obedience and respect of its subjects. It is also admitted, that a people, when it has no Government, is free to adopt one form of Government, in preference to another, to give or to refuse allegiance to that which is proposed. In accordance with the above first principle the people of this country had obeyed and respected the authority to which the circumstances which surrounded its infancy compelled it to be subject.

A company of adventurers known as the "Hudson Bay Company," and invested with certain powers, granted by His Majesty (Charles II), established itself in Rupert's Land, and in the North-West Territory, for trading purposes only. This Company, consisting of many persons, required a certain constitution. But as there was a question of commerce only, their constitution was framed in reference thereto. Yet, since there was at that time no Government to see to the interest of a people already existing in the country, it became necessary for judicial affairs to have recourse to the officers of the Hudson Bay Company. This inaugurated that species of government which, slightly modified by subsequent circumstances, ruled this country up to recent date.

Whereas, that Government, thus accepted, was far from answering to the wants of the people, and became more and more so, as the population increased in numbers, and as the country was developed, and commerce extended, until the present day, when it commands a place amongst the colonies; and this people, ever actuated by the above-mentioned principles, had generously supported the aforesaid Government, and gave to it a faithful allegiance, when, contrary to the law of nations, in March, 1869, that said Government surrendered and transferred to Canada all the rights which it had, or pretended to have, in this Territory, by transactions with which the people were considered unworthy to be made acquainted.

And, whereas, it is also generally admitted that a people is at liberty to establish any form of government it may consider suited to its wants, as soon as the power to which it was subject abandons it, or attempts to subjugate it, without its consent to a foreign power; and maintain that no right can be transferred to such foreign power. Now, therefore, first, we, the representatives of the people, in Council assembled in Upper Fort Garry, on the 24th day of November, 1869, after having invoked the God of Nations, relying on these fundamental moral principles, solemnly declare, in the name of our constituents, and in our own names, before God and man, that, from the day on which the Government we had always respected abandoned us, by transferring to a strange power the sacred authority confided to it, the people of Rupert's Land and the North-West became free and exempt from all allegiance to the said Government. Second. That we refuse to recognize the authority of Canada, which pretends to have a right to coerce us, and impose upon us a despotic form of government still more contrary to our rights and interests as British subjects, than was that Government to which we had subjected our-selves, through necessity up to recent date. Thirdly. That, by sending an expedition on the 1ˢᵗ November, ult., charged to drive back Mr. William McDougall and his companions, coming in the name of Canada, to rule us with the rod of despotism, without previous notification to that effect, we have acted conformably to that sacred right which commands every citizen to offer energetic opposition to pre-vent this country from being enslaved. Fourth. That we continue, and shall continue, to oppose, with all our strength, the establishing of the 'Canadian authority in our country, under the announced form; and, in case of persistence on the part of the Canadian Government to enforce its obnoxious policy upon us by force of arms, we protest before-hand against such an unjust and unlawful course; and we declare the said Canadian Government responsible, before God and men, for the innumerable evils which may be caused by so unwarrantable a course. Be it known, therefore, to the world in general and to the Canadian Government in particular, that, as we have always heretofore successfully defended our country in frequent wars with the neighbouring tribes of Indians, who are now on friendly relations with us, we are firmly resolved in future, not less than in the past, to repel all invasions from whatsoever quarter they may come; and, further more, we do declare and proclaim, in the name of the people of Rupert's Land and the North-West, that we have, on the said 24th day of November, 1869, above mentioned, established a Provisional Government, and hold it to be the only and lawful authority now in existence in Rupert's Land and the North-West which claims the obedience and respect of the people; that, meanwhile, we hold our-selves in readiness to enter in such negotiations with the Canadian Government as may be favourable for the good government and prosperity of this people. In support of this declaration, relying on the protection of Divine

Providence, we mutually pledge ourselves, on oath, our lives, our fortunes, and our sacred honor, to each other.

Issued at Fort Garry, this Eighth day of December, in the year of our Lord, One thousand eight hundred and sixty-nine.

John Bruce, Pres. Louis Riel, Sec.

"Well," Guillaume said, folding the paper up and tucking it into his pouch, "let's hope this will see an end to the prejudice and persecution we have endured at the hands of the English. They are not our overlords, and they must now surely see that the Mètis, along with the Cree, the Saulteax, and the Souix, have established self-governance of their own lands long before Rupert's Land was established. Perhaps now, they will negotiate in good faith and honour our scripts and our right to our language and beliefs."

"We can only hope," Baptiste agreed.

That man! I see him!" Archie grabbed Guillaume's arm, pointing to the edges of the milling crowd.

"What man? The one you saw going into Ashmore's house?" Guillaume scooped the slight figure up and held him so he could see over the heads of the men around them.

"Yes, yes. He was right there..." Archie scanned the crowd. "There! He just went between those buildings. I'd know that coat anywhere."

Guillaume set Archie down and with his friends in tow, shouldered his way through the crowd. By the time they reached the edge, their quarry was nowhere in sight.

"He went down there." Archie pointed between two buildings and started forward.

"Hold." Guillaume caught him by the coat collar. "He may be armed, he certainly does not wish to be observed." He entered the narrow space, knife in his hand. "Nothing." He shook his head and returned to his friends. "What would one of Ashmore's servants be doing here?"

"Spying." Pierre spat on the ground.

"Up to no good," Baptiste agreed.

"One day soon his luck will run out, and I will have him in my hands," Guillaume vowed.

"I will ask the trapper to see if his sister Josie can tell us the names of the two man servants and if she has seen or heard anything that might interest us," Pierre promised.

"Be sure she knows to be careful. I wouldn't wish any harm to come to her and we already know this man is capable of murder," Guillaume insisted.

"Come along. Perhaps we will find who we seek at the saloon." Hugh O'Lone slung an arm around his companion's shoulders.

"You should return to the cabin and apologize to Fèlicitè for running off on her." Guillaume fixed Archie with a glare. "You can walk with us as far as the cabins."

"Can't I come to the saloon? It's not like I haven't been in there working and stuff," Archie protested. "I bet I could recognize the man before you would."

"He might have a point, Will," Hugh said.

"Cabin," Guillaume ordered. "I will feel better knowing there is someone to guard Fèlicitè and the boys. You know where the rifle and ammunition are kept."

Archie straightened his bony shoulders and fell into step beside the men. "Of course, if you need me to guard the cabin, I can do that," he agreed.

Guillaume hid a smile behind his beard and squeezed the young man's shoulder.

* * *

The mass at St. Boniface was overfull on Friday December 10, 1869. Excitement and a sense of expectation rippled through the congregation as Riel stood and declared that everyone in attendance was invited to celebrate the creation of the provisional government at three that very afternoon.

Guillaume, Pierre, Baptiste, and Hugh were kept busy with the preparations. Fortunately, the weather had improved, and the temperature was surprisingly mild. Wisps and clumps of fog rose from the river, swirling among the crowd in ghostly fingers and shadows. It lent an air of sanctity and approval by the ancestors to the proceedings.

The quadrangle of Fort Garry was full to overflowing. Father Dugas had the St. Boniface Boys' Bugle Band in full voice, blaring out old French hymns and folk songs. They lapsed into silence when Father Ritchot stepped forward. The Father offered up a heartfelt prayer. When he concluded, Guillaume and Pierre came forward with the new flag, a *fleur de lis* and a shamrock on a pristine white background and hoisted it up the flagpole. In a welcome gesture of luck and acceptance, a wind came up and snapped the new flag into full view high above the heads of the crowd.

Guillaume looked up at the new flag bravely flying and offered up a silent prayer of his own for good luck and the longevity of the new government. The bugle band broke into another bright tune while the crowd cheered in jubilation. Volleys of gunfire rent the air, blasting into the sky, shattering the remnants of the fog.

O'Lone and Baptiste assisted in hauling a huge kettle of liquor with a goblet attached. Every member of those gathered who wished to drank and toasted the realization of the Mètis' dream. A government that would protect their rights and their land. Guillaume joined in with the rest as they roared three cheers for the provisional government, Louis Riel and the other leaders and concluded with one for the brass band. He moved through the crowd to join Fèlicitè and the boys, grinning at her as they joined in the three groans for the deposed police chief James Mulligan in the Fort Garry jail. In his mind he also directed the groans at Mair, Schultz, and the others from Fort Schultz who were safely in the jail cells as well and could most certainly hear the celebrations.

Louis Riel mounted the steps and the crowd fell as silent as a huge boisterous crowd could. Riel was a charismatic and passionate speaker, Guillaume and Fèlicitè were too far to the back to hear much of what was said. Guillaume hoisted Alexandre to his shoulders and Fèlicitè did the same with Ètienne. Archie wormed his way to the front of the crowd, returning only when Riel concluded his speech.

"What did he say?" Fèlicitè asked, setting Ètienne on the ground, but keeping hold of his hand.

"A lot of stuff. He went on about us remembering we are still loyal to the Crown, he talked a lot in French and Cree that I didn't understand, but I think he was just repeating what he said in English," Archie reported. "O'Lone says you and Pierre and Baptiste are to go find him, they're planning on taking a picture and you should be in it."

"You stay here with Fèlicitè and the boys. I need to know they are safe in this crowd. Can I trust you to do that?"

Archie nodded and took Alexandre's hand. "I'll take everyone home when they're ready."

"I'll see you there then." Guillaume winked at Fèlicitè before he hurried away. It took some manoeuvering to reach the place where the provisional government members were gathering. Hugh O'Lone made his way into the fray, ending up crouching by Louis' right, his arm resting casually on Riel's knee. Pierre and Guillaume stood in the background behind the other men, staying out of range of the camera lens. By unspoken consent, the two men sought to avoid the spotlight. As soon as the gathering broke up, Guillaume hurried toward his cabin. He needed to speak with Archie once more. Pierre went off in search of his trapper friend, and hopefully, the man's sister Josie. The crackle of paper in his pouch reminded him of the proclamation he had shoved inside. Time to read that more closely later. For now, it was more important to see if Archie could remember anything else that might lead to the murderer, or murderers, as Guillaume was beginning to think might be the case.

Chapter Fourteen

The unseasonably mild weather of a few days before was a fleeting memory on the afternoon Guillaume set out to meet with Pierre and Xavier. Huddled inside the buffalo coat, he stamped his feet to remove the snow and pushed open the cabin door. He paused after shutting the door to let his eyes adjust to the dim interior.

"Guillaume, come join us by the fire." Pierre poured his friend a mug of tea laced with whisky.

"*Merci*." He pulled the chair closer to the hearth and accepted the warm mug. "Xavier," he acknowledged the third occupant of the cabin.

"Mousseau," the trapper replied, studying the tall man over the edge of his mug.

"Is there anything new?" Guillaume rested his mug on his knee, leaning toward Xavier. "We have not put your sister in any danger, I hope."

"Not as far as I know. She should be along in a few minutes."

Guillaume straightened suddenly. "She's not coming here..."

"Peace, Guillaume. Lady Ashmore sends her on errands into the village almost daily, Josie will be careful not to be seen coming or leaving here," Xavier promised. "*Ma soeur* is much more clever than the *femme anglaise* gives her credit for."

Before Guillaume could protest further a tentative knock sounded on the door. Pierre rose and ushered the slight woman into the cabin and led her toward the fire. Guillaume got to his feet and offered his chair to her. With a shy smile, Josie set her satchel by her feet and perched on the edge of the chair.

"Jo, this is Guillaume Mousseau, Pierre you already know," Xavier introduced his sister. "Guillaume, *ma soeur* Josie."

"*Bonjour, monsieur*," Josie tipped her head toward Guillaume.

The action revealed she was much younger than he had supposed. The girl could hardly be more than sixteen. He squatted on his heels in front of her, gazing into her face. "*Mademoiselle*, Josie, what can you tell me of the Ashmore house?"

Josie glanced at her brother and swallowed before she spoke. "There is Lord and Lady Ashmore, of course. The cook, Lady Ashmore's maid, Amelia who came with her from England, two man servants, Oliver and Gregory, and myself. On special occasions when they are entertaining or hosting company, they employ my cousin and my younger sister to help, but they are not there on a regular basis." She ducked her head and twisted her hands in her lap.

The two man servants, this Oliver and Gregory, was one of them sent into town recently on any errands?" Guillaume clenched his fists on his thighs.

Josie nodded. "It is usually Gregory who Lord Ashmore sends on his errands. He seems to trust him more than Oliver," she glanced up at Guillaume, "perhaps because he is the older of the two."

"Does this Gregory own a dark green jacket that has needed repairs lately?" Guillaume pressed her.

Josie's head jerked up, eyes wide and startled. "*Oui*, yes. A week or so ago, Lady Ashmore directed me to sew a rip in his coat and to replace a button on the sleeve."

Guillaume controlled the spurt of excitement curling through him. "What type of button, Josie," he kept his voice calm.

"*Quoi*? Does it matter?"

"Very much. What type of button, Josie?"

She closed her eyes for a moment, a frown of concentration furrowing her brow. Nodding, her eyes opened, gleaming in the firelight. "It was a silver one, Lord Ashmore insists the men have silver buttons on the coats they wear when on duty."

Guillaume's fingers sought his pouch, pulling out the object he had taken from his sister's dead hand. "Is it like this one?" He handed it to her.

Hesitantly, Josie took the silver button. She turned it over in her palm with a trembling finger. "How did you get this?" she whispered, large eyes on Guillaume's face.

"Is it the same as the one missing from this Gregory's jacket?"

Josie nodded; gaze drawn back to the button glinting in her palm. "It most certainly could be. But how do you have this? Lord Ashmore keeps a small supply of them which he has sent from England. Lady Ashmore keeps them locked in her special jewel case."

Guillaume met Pierre's gaze and gave an almost imperceptible shake of his head. Xavier leaned forward, elbows on his knees.

"It is important, this button?" Xavier inquired. "Are you sure it is the same as the one you sewed on the jacket?" he addressed his sister.

"*Oui*. Look, it has the Ashmore coat of arms on it. I could not be mistaken," Josie insisted. "How do you have one in your possession?" She frowned at Guillaume, then a swift progression of expression crossed her features as realization dawned on her. "This is the missing button from the coat, isn't it? Where did you find it?"

"Where I found it is of no importance to you, *mademoiselle*. It is better I think for all of us if you do not know." Guillaume retrieved the button from her hand. He touched the ring in his pouch and brought it out into the light. "I found this in the mud near where my sisters lay. Do you recognize it?" He passed it to her, the gold glinting in the firelight.

She turned it over in her palm with the forefinger of her other hand before handing it back to him. "I don't recall ever seeing anything like this before." She handed it back to him.

Guillaume tucked the ring back in his pouch. "If you remember anything else, please send word to me."

Josie nodded, got to her feet and collected her satchel. "I must go, if I am gone much longer Lady Ashmore will be angry and ask questions I do not wish to answer."

Guillaume walked with her to the door. "My thanks, *Mademoiselle* Josie. Your help is much appreciated. If you are ever in need, please do not hesitate to contact myself or Pierre. We are in your debt" He opened the door but kept her from passing. "It would be best if you mentioned this meeting and what passed here to no one."

The look she levelled at him set him back on his heels.

"I am not an *imbécile, monsieur.*" Josie swept out the door, giving him a withering glance over her shoulder.

Xavier rose as well. "I will follow her and be sure she arrives safely back."

"I think that would be wise," Pierre agreed. "*Merci*, for your assistance."

"I have no more love for the English interlopers than you. It is my pleasure if I can be of assistance in revealing their true nature." Xavier disappeared out the door.

Guillaume returned to the fire, sitting across from Pierre, and picking up his neglected mug of tea and whisky. "We have a name now, and some damning evidence. The question is, how to go forward."

"We could drag the man before the council of the provisional government and ask them for a decision and a punishment," Pierre suggested.

Guillaume snorted. "I doubt Ashmore would allow us to remove the man from his residence without a fight. *Non*, I think we must wait and watch and when next the man is sent out on an errand...perhaps he will be waylaid."

Pierre nodded. "How will we keep a watch though. We both have duties we cannot ignore..."

Guillaume smiled. "The activity will be better suited to Archie. He can lurk about like any one of the ragged street children. He will fit right in, as he used to be one of them, and I know he still keeps in contact with some of them. I think he will find it amusing to recruit a little gang of his own to help him keep watch."

"Will he keep his mouth shut though? We can't have any whisper of our need to get our hands on Ashmore's man or he will be on his guard," Pierre cautioned.

"Archie will do as I ask. He is clever and will figure out a story to satisfy anyone he recruits. He is nothing if not loyal to me."

"Pierre grinned. "He is also besotted with Fèlicitè. Perhaps you should have her impress on Archie the need for complete secrecy regarding our true objective."

Guillaume shot him a surprised glance and then nodded. "That may not be a bad idea. I will discuss it with Fèlicitè." He got to his feet, setting the now empty mug on the hearthstone. "Speaking of obligations, I must go attend to mine. I will see you later at O'Lone's?"

"I'm planning on going by for a drink and something to eat, I have no heart to cook for myself," Pierre admitted.

Guillaume paused on his way out the door. "Why not come and eat with us? I need to spend some time with the boys, and I know Fèlicitè will have enough for one more. You know you are always welcome."

"I will take you up on that." Pierre shook his head with a rueful grin. "You should marry that girl, Guillaume. There is talk you know...and I think Baptiste and her *maman* are hopeful."

Guillaume snorted and refrained from commenting as he went out, closing the door behind him with a thump. Pierre deposited the empty mugs on the table by the wall that served as his storage area. He missed Marie-Anne most at times like this, her quiet movements, a hand trailing down his arm or shoulder as she passed. The firelight flickering on her sable hair when she sat by the hearth, head bent over some mending or embroidery. His fingers caressed the bright sash at his waist, her love alive in every stitch.

Shoving the thoughts aside, he banked the fire, pulled on his buffalo coat, and stepped outside. His steps took him toward the village, walking helped him think and a quick reconnaissance of Ashmore's residence and surround didn't seem like a bad idea. His hands clenched inside the deerskin mitts imagining them wrapped around this Gregory's throat.

* * *

"*Entrè, entrè*," Guillaume answered Pierre's knock on the cabin door.

Pierre stepped into the firelit room, the rich, redolent scent of whatever was bubbling in the cauldron over the glowing coals of the hearth bringing warmth to his chest. And a wish for a return of the nights he would come home to find a similar scene in his own cabin with Anne-Marie smiling by the hearth. He shook his head and hung his outerwear on a hook by the door.

"*Accueillir*," Fèlicitè greeted him. The table was set with five clay plates and mugs. Small bone spoons lay beside the younger boys' places. "The rubaboo is in the pot. I must go and help *Maman* with some things."

223

She crossed the room and wrapped her outer clothing snugly around her. With one hand on the door, she cast a glance at Archie. "You will remember what we talked about, *oui*?"

Archie shook his head solemnly. "I will, Fèlicitè. I promised."

"See that you do." With a decisive nod, she whisked out the door.

Guillaume rose and barred the door before ladling rubaboo onto the boys' plates. Alexandre helped Ètienne into the taller chair and put the bone spoon in his fist. Archie brought a loaf of bread from the cupboard along with a sharp knife which he used to cut a generous slice for each boy. He cut a piece for himself and the two men before filling the remaining three plates with stew.

"What did Fèlicitè speak with you about? Has there been a problem?" Guillaume gave Archie a sideways glance.

"No, no." He dipped his head and his cheeks reddened. "She reminded me that I shouldn't repeat anything you speak about and how important it is that I don't run on at the mouth about private things."

Guillaume nodded, his mouth full of stew, he mopped up some gravy with his bread. Swallowing, he fixed Archie with a stern gaze. "When supper is over, I have something to discuss with you. Something I need your help with."

"Of course. Anything." Archie nodded, his long hair falling over his face. He brushed it back with an impatient hand. "What do you need me to do?"

"Later." Guillaume nodded slightly at the two younger boys. To distract Alexandre's attention, he continued. "Are you comfortable watching my nephews after? Pierre and I have some business we need to take care of." He noted Alexandre lost interest in the conversation and turned his attention back to his stew and helping Ètienne eat.

"I can take care of them, sure." Archie paused, "Is Fèlicitè coming back soon?"

"Fèlicitè is needed at home. She will be here in the morning. Are you sure you will be okay on your own for a while?"

Archie straightened his thin shoulders. "Yes, sir. We'll be fine." He smiled at the two younger boys and used a rag to wipe Ètienne's face.

"We will talk after I return. I will not be late." Guillaume wiped the last of the gravy with the crust of bread and rose, taking his plate to the dry sink by the cupboard.

Pierre followed suit, and the two men left with a reminder from Guillaume for Archie to bar the door behind them. The two men strode through the twilight along the near deserted track. As they neared the hub of buildings in the village proper foot traffic increased. They passed by Ashmore's residence on the corner of Fire Engine Street, Guillaume paused and gazed at the lighted windows. Pierre laid a hand on his arm.

"There is nothing to be gained by standing here and if someone sees us it may well give Ashmore something to complain about."

"I wish nothing more than to break down that door and drag the man into the street." Guillaume ground his teeth.

"Which man? Ashmore or his servant?" Pierre grinned and tugged on his friend's arm. "*Aller*, let us go. My throat is dry."

"Either man, if you must know. If it is the servant who did the deed, it was most certainly his master who commanded it." Guillaume allowed himself to be moved along the street, glaring over his shoulder.

"Most likely true, but we must move carefully. The provisional government council won't back our actions if we move without some proof."

They passed Monchamp's saloon a bit further down the street, light and noise spilling out the doors. Guillaume's footsteps slowed and he regarded the establishment with a thoughtful gaze. Pierre stopped and waited, impatient to continue on to O'Lone's.

"I wonder if we should perhaps pass some time in there?" Guillaume mused. "It is close to Ashmore's and not a place we usually gather." He moved toward the doors.

Shrugging, Pierre followed. Inside, they pushed their way to the bar. Whisky in hand, they turned, leaned on the bar, and surveyed the room. Pierre struck up a conversation with the man beside him who was already in his cups.

"I was hoping to find a friend of mine here...have you seen Gregory this evening?"

The Englishman blinked and squinted bleary eyes at Pierre. "Gregory?" He moved a step away from Pierre when he realized the man wasn't a fellow countryman.

"Yes, Gregory. He works for Miles Ashmore."

"Oh, one of the servants? Can't say as I have." The Englishman turned his back on Pierre and Guillaume.

"I doubt we will have much luck here," Pierre spoke close to Guillaume's ear to be heard above the babble of voices.

"A moment, longer." Guillaume continued to scan the gathered men over the rim of his glass. A half hour and two whiskys later he concluded Pierre was in the right. Setting his glass on the bar, he shouldered his way to the door.

In the relative quiet of the street, the men continued to King Street, walking with brisk strides past Dutch George's store and Colonel Dennis' surveyor office. The latter looking abandoned. Stepping into O'Lone's the noise and light washed over them. Pierre stopped to exchange gossip with some men at a table while Guillaume headed for the bar and a word with Hugh who was currently pulling pints from a keg behind the long bar.

"Hugh." Guillaume put some coin on the bar. "Two pints."

"Will, good to see you." Hugh finished pulling the pints he was working on and slid them down the polished surface to the far end where eager hands caught them.

"Any news?" Guillaume leaned over the surface and lowered his voice.

Hugh scooped up the coin before depositing the pints on the counter. "Nothing of what you're looking for, I'm afraid. Although," he ran a hand over his rough beard, "the man you're interested in hasn't been in here for quite a while. Used to show up at least twice a week, but in the last few weeks, haven't seen hide nor hair of 'em." He winked and laid a finger up the side of his nose.

Guillaume nodded and took a swig of his beer. Pierre sidled up beside him and claimed the other pint.

"Hugh." Pierre saluted the man with his beer before drinking deep. "I had a word with a few of the boys when I came in. Seems our quarry has gone to ground, no one has seen him in the past week."

"That is what Hugh tells me as well. This may prove more difficult than we believed. He must have got spooked when we tracked him after Archie spotted him."

Hugh moved off down the bar to serve his customers. Thomas Scott's imprisonment had left him without a bartender. Not that anyone missed the man's abrasive manners. Pierre and Guillaume lingered over their pints, surveying the raucous crowd, eavesdropping on snatches of conversation without learning anything of what they were searching for. Leaving the saloon, Guillaume parted ways with Pierre and strode off into the darkness. There was still the conversation with Archie to be conducted. It looked more and more like Archie and his hopefully recruited gang of urchins was going to be their best hope of getting their hands on Ashmore's servant man.

Chapter Fifteen

Guillaume knocked on the door, shifting from foot to foot in the chill night air.

"Archie, *c'est moi. Ouvrè la porte.*" The welcome sound of wood scraping against wood proceeded the door opening a slit revealing Archie's pale face.

The boy stepped back to allow Guillaume entry, setting the rifle down beside the door as he did so. Guillaume patted him on the shoulder in approval before replacing the bar across the door. He glanced toward the lumps under the blankets where his nephews slept, before sinking into the chair by the fire where Archie joined him, settling in the opposite seat. The young man leaned forward, elbows on his bony knees.

"What do you need to talk to me about?" Archie's low voice betrayed the tension he was attempting to hide.

"Do you still hang out with any friends in the village when you aren't looking after the boys?"

"Well, sure...some of them," Archie admitted. "Do you not want me to do that?"

"*Non, non.* The opposite. I need you to recruit as many of your friends as you can trust, I mean really trust."

"To do what?" Archie frowned. "I don't want nothin' to do with anything that'll get me in trouble."

"Nothing that should get you into any trouble. I need you and your friends to just hang around in the village like you do now, but while you're doing that keep an eye out for the man, Gregory, that we're very sure is the same man you saw the night my sisters were murdered."

"I can do that...what should I do if we see him?"

"It might be best to work in pairs, then one of you can keep eyes on the man while the other comes to find me or Pierre. Preferably me."

Archie breathed a sigh of relief. "I don't think that should be too hard. So long as you don't want any of us to actually stop the man." He shivered. "I don't want to end up in the river," he muttered.

"That is not something I want either," Guillaume assured him. "How long do you think it will take you to round up some friends to help with this?"

Archie shrugged. "I can start in the morning, but it would help if I could offer them something...for their trouble, you know? Most of them are living rough, kipping in some of the abandoned buildings, scavenging for food..."

Guillaume leaned back in his chair, eyes on the glowing coals at the base of the blaze. "I can offer them either pemican, and other foods that will last, maybe a place to sleep in the shed with the horse. It isn't much but it is safe and there is straw in the loft and I'm sure we can spare some blankets. Failing that, I am willing to offer some coin, but I'd rather not do that if I don't have to. Keep that as a last resort and only if you think the recruit is worth it. Understand?"

Archie grinned. "Yeah, that will work. I can think of about four fellows off the top of my head who will be interested."

"*Bien.*" Guillaume got up and banked the fire. "Remember to tell them they have no need to approach the man themselves, just watch for him and send for me if they find him in the village or around. Pierre and I will take care of it from there. Let me know when your gang is in place. Go on to bed now, Archie. Morning comes early." He patted the young man on the shoulder and sought his own bed.

* * *

Guillaume shoved open the shed door and gathered up a coil of wire, hammer, and some nails. Emerging, he closed the door and squinted at the brilliant orb of the sun in the arctic blue sky. Shifting the bag on his shoulder, he set off toward Baptiste's. Smoke curled from the chimney of his cabin, Fèlicitè

232

must be either boiling water to wash the boys' clothes or perhaps waiting for the fire to die down so she could bake bannock in the hot coals. He grinned, Baptiste's daughter certainly managed his house well, and she was an excellent cook. The grin faded as his feet took him toward his destination. Perhaps he should consider speaking to Baptiste about the girl. She was pretty in her own quiet way, and if the chatter Archie and Alex filled his ears with was true, Fèlicitè would not be adverse to such an arrangement. Practical matters aside, it would be nice to have someone to come home to and to warm his bed on the long winter nights.

He snorted and quickened his pace. Time enough to think on those things once he'd dragged the bastard who murdered his sisters into the hands of what law there was and seen justice done. A muscle twitched in his jaw; Pierre favoured taking the man to the council of the soon to be declared provincial government while Guillaume much preferred the idea of beating the man senseless. Clubbing him on the head as he'd done to Marguerite and Marie-Anne, and then dumping him in the cold fast flowing waters of the Red River. He considered for a moment, maybe the Riviere Salè might be better. It was more remote and there would be far less chance of anyone going to the man's rescue.

"Guillaume, out here," Baptiste hailed him from the shed behind his cabin. "Your help is much appreciated. The fence near the river is down again."

"Baptiste. A bright sunny day for such a chore," he joked.

The other man huffed and clapped Guillaume on the back. "Let's get to it. The sooner we get that section of fence shored up, the sooner we can be warm."

The two men trudged off through the snow and followed the fence line toward the river. Arriving at the trouble spot they set about tightening wire and straightening the posts titled by the wind. Stopping to wipe the frost clinging to his beard, Guillaume caught movement out of the corner of his vision.

"Guillaume, Guillaume!" Archie's voice carried on the December air.

"A moment, Baptiste. It's Archie. I must see what he wants." Guillaume set down his tools and strode to meet the running figure.

Archie reached him and bent double, hands on his knees as he dragged breath into his lungs. He gripped Guillaume's arm and struggled to speak.

Guillaume stuck a hand inside his coat, pulled out the flask he carried and handed it to Archie. "Take drink and try to calm down."

Archie grabbed the flask and took a big swallow, which he promptly spewed back out in a fine spray. He shoved the flask back at Guillaume, and coughing, wiped his swimming eyes. "It's him," he managed to get out. "Sam's following 'im, right now. I ran to come get you." He grabbed Guillaume's arm. "Come on, before we lose 'im or 'e gets back to the house."

"You're sure it's the right man?" Guillaume kept a tight hold on the excitement building in his gut.

"Yeah, c'mon!" Archie started dragging the older man back toward the cabins.

"Baptiste! I must go take care of something. I will be back when I can." Guillaume waved at his friend and followed Archie who was tugging impatiently at his arm. "Where did you leave him?"

"Saw him down by the Company store. It's him alright. I got close enough to be sure, and I'll never forget that stink of whatchacallit...lavender. I told Sam to stay with him and came as fast as I could to get you." Archie broke into a run, struggling now to keep up with Guillaume's longer stride.

"Does Pierre know?"

"No. Should I have gone to him first, seeing as he's in the village?"

"Just as well you came to me. Let's hope Sam doesn't lose the man before we get there." Guillaume increased his stride, leaving Archie to keep up as best he could. Entering the village, Guillaume slowed his headlong pace and contented himself with a ground eating walk. Archie caught up with him and pointed down the street to a spot where a laneway cut off of King Street near

Dutch George's store that led down to the two churches.

"There. I can see Sam and a few of the boys. Your man must be inside the store."

"We'll see. Well done, Archie. Tell your gang to come by the cabin later, if I get my hands on this Gregory there will be a bonus for them." Guillaume jogged toward the little knot of four young men. "Where is he?"

"He went into Dutch George's a while ago, but he ain't come out yet?" Sam reported.

Guillaume frowned at the building. "Is anyone watching the back of the store?"

"Yes, sir. I sent Harry round the back, just in case your man decided to do a runner." Sam gave a decisive nod of his head.

Guillaume squeezed his shoulder. "Well done. I think I'll just take a peek in the store. You men stay on watch and if he gets away follow him. Try to slow him down if you can, but don't do anything that attracts too much attention."

The small gathering nodded and assumed nonchalant positions outside the store, a few of them smoking while two of them flipped copper bits at the wall. Guillaume stepped up onto the wooden porch and shoved the door open. He stopped to let his eyes adjust to the change in light. Sunlight streamed through the front windows, but the rest of the store was full of shadows. He nodded to the man behind the counter to the left of the door and scanned his surroundings. A couple of older men sat by the pot belly stove near the big pickle barrel. Guillaume moved past them and wandered deeper into the store. Two women examined the bolts of cloth spread out on another counter. Guillaume recognized Josie and Lady Ashmore, he caught Josie's attention and acknowledged her tiny shake of the head. She cast her eyes toward the alcove in the far corner of the building, before turning her attention back to her employer who sent her off to fetch George. Lady Ashmore remained by the cloth, running her gloved fingers over something Guillaume couldn't see. He drifted toward the alcove, keeping one eye on Lady Ashmore. Though she never turned her head in his direction, he caught her giving him and the alcove sideways glances and her fingers closed tightly on the bolt of cloth.

His pulse raced in anticipation. The nearer he drew to the alcove, the more the woman fidgeted. Guillaume's fingers itched. Gregory must be within his grasp. With a swift movement he blocked the entry to the alcove and searched the small space. He poked behind the stacks of merchandise stored there, finding nothing. His instincts told him he was close, but where was the man? There were only so many places to hide in such a small space. Pushing aside an array of long handled tools his hand landed on a bit of wall that gave way under his fingers. Cursing under his breath, he bent down and discovered the small trap door with the hook unlatched. Straightening, he backed out into the store. Lady Ashmore tilted her nose in the air as he moved by her, but he noticed the atmosphere of tension that surrounded her when he entered the alcove was gone. She must be hiding something, shielding her servant, and through him, her murdering husband. Long strides took him toward the door. So close, so close....

"Guillaume, this way." Archie met him outside the door, fairly vibrating with excitement. "Back here." He led the way behind the store where the snow showed signs of some sort of scuffle.

"I lost him. He got away out the back." Guillaume clenched his hands. "What is back here?"

Archie gave a low whistle which was answered by another. "This way."

He marched off disappearing behind the stockade that encompassed a good portion of the back of the store. Guillaume followed, coming around the corner to find three of Archie's gang sitting on Lord Ashmore's man servant. He stopped in his tracks and surveyed the scene. The man on the ground lifted his head, mouth open to beseech Guillaume for help. Recognition flooded across his face, quickly replaced by terror while the colour leached out of his features. He dropped his face back into the cradle of his shoulder.

Guillaume gripped the back of the man's collar and twisted the coat and the shirt beneath it tight against his neck. "Let him up."

The three young men scrambled off the prone figure, swiping the snow off their clothes. They joined Archie and Sam, forming a circle around Guillaume and the man they supposed was Gregory. Guillaume hauled the shorter man to his feet and shook him.

"You will tell me what you know," he growled.

"Gregory? Gregory, where has that man got to?" Lady Ashmore's voice trembled with unspoken anxiety came from the street.

"Not a sound," Guillaume warned the man in his grasp, shoving him back to the ground where three of the boys promptly sat on him again. He nodded in the direction of the street, around the building, sending Sam and Archie to stand guard there and sound a warning if anyone approached.

"Josie, Josie! Do go around the back and see if perhaps Gregory has been waylaid," Lady Ashmore commanded, her voice hard and cold. "Go on, girl. Move."

Her words were followed by a stifled female yelp. Archie glanced back over his shoulder, looking to Guillaume for direction while tentative footsteps approached from the street.

"See what she wants," Guillaume hissed. "Don't let her see anything she shouldn't."

Archie nodded and stepped forward to intercept Josie. "Josie, what are you doing here?"

"Madam sent me to see if her man servant was back here," Josie's voice quavered, her gaze darting toward the cluster of people surrounding Guillaume who had his back to her.

Archie moved to block her line of sight. "There ain't nobody back here but us. No need to look any further."

Josie craned her neck attempting to see around him. "Did you get him? Gregory?" she whispered. "Her Ladyship won't like it, but I'm glad if it's so."

Archie took her arm and turned her back toward the street. "The less you know, the less trouble you can get into. Go back and tell Lady Ashmore there was no one back here. Go." He gave her a little push.

"Josephine!" The imperious summons came from the corner of the store. "Josephine, did you find Gregory?"

"Go." Archie pushed her a little harder.

"Coming, m'am." With one last glance toward Guillaume, she gathered up her skirts and picked her way back to the street. "There was nothing back there, m'am. No sign of anyone."

"He must have gone already, then. We'll see when we get home. Come along, girl. Pick up the parcels and be quick about it." Lady Ashmore, trailed by a laden down Josie, sailed into view along King Street.

Breathing a sigh of relief, Archie nodded at Sam and the two joined the rest of the gang surrounding Guillaume and his captive. "They're gone," Archie reported.

"*Bien.*" He nudged the prone man with his toe. "Go and find Hugh and Pierre. Ask Hugh if he would call the council together, tell him I have found the man who murdered my sisters. Take one of your friends with you so it will go faster."

Archie nodded, grabbed Sam's arm and the pair took off at a run. Guillaume turned his attention to the shivering Englishman at his feet. "Let him up," he growled. The three boys sitting on the man got up, but the prisoner made no effort to rise. Guillaume leaned down and hauled him to his feet by the scruff of his coat collar.

"Now, we will have a small talk, you and I." He shook the slighter man hard enough to snap his head back and forth. "You murdered my sisters who have never done anything to harm you or yours. I would like some answers." He shook him again.

"I didn't...I didn't..." Gregory stammered, his eyes wide and wild, darting toward the opening to the street.

"You did. I have a witness who saw you that night, heard you strike them down and saw you slinking back through the night. What I need to know is why? *Pourquoi*? Why those two women? I cannot believe it was a coincidence. You went out on a cold snowy night and tracked them down. Did you follow them from Ashmore's after they asked for help for the child?"

Gregory shook his head, a trickle of blood running down his cheek from a scrape by his temple. "I didn't," he started to say and then clamped his mouth shut. "I have nothing to say to the likes of you." His endeavor to look contemptuous failed miserably.

"We could make 'em talk," Henry, one of Archie's friends offered, smacking his fist into the palm of his other hand.

"We could, but I think we need to let the council handle this. Louis' provisional government is in charge now and we must be careful not to undermine their authority." Or run afoul of the Englishmen either, he finished in his head. Taking a length of rawhide from his pouch he bound Gregory's hands behind him. With the young men surrounding him, Guillaume marched the Englishman through the streets to Fort Garry. Archie and Sam joined them on the way.

"I found Hugh and he's calling in the council, he sent a runner to the fort, so they know you're coming and will have a cell ready for him." Archie nodded at the bedraggled Englishman, his fine wool coat covered in snow and bits of leaves and sticks.

"*Bien*. They can convince him to speak. I wish to hear from his lips why he committed such a crime."

"They were nothing, dirty savages, nothing to make such a fuss over." Gregory straightened up, fire in his blue eyes. "That pair had no business coming to Lord and Lady Ashmore's residence, befouling the doorstep with their presence." He subsided at Guillaume's hiss of rage.

Archie darted in and kicked the prisoner hard in the knee causing him to stumble.

"Enough." Guillaume hauled him upright again and twisted the neck cloth tight around the scrawny neck. "You will not speak ill of my sisters. Your precious Lord Ashmore is the father of my sister's children which gave her every right to ask his assistance."

Spitting blood from where he'd bitten his lip, Gregory glared as best he could at his captor. "An insult, a huge insult to her Ladyship. Having her nose rubbed in the evidence of her husband's disgusting behaviour. Is it any wonder she refuses him her bedroom?" His face paled and he clamped his jaw shut as if he realized he'd said too much.

"You will not speak ill of my sisters," Guillaume repeated and shoved him forward. The sooner he could get the man to Fort Garry and turn him over the better.

* * *

"Where is he?" Pierre grabbed Guillaume's arm and spun him around. His

243

face was red with exertion, frost dripped from his beard in the heat of the room. He'd obviously run the whole way from the village to the fort.

"In the cells," Guillaume answered. He gestured toward the chair beside him.

"You caught the English bastard? The one young Archie saw?" Pierre sank into the chair, his breathing returning to normal.

Guillaume nodded. "Shopping with Ashmore's wife at Dutch George's." He paused and frowned. "Josie was with them. I wonder why the lady's maid wasn't with her. From what the girl said when we talked to her, she never gets out of the kitchen."

Pierre grinned. "I heard the lady's maid is in danger of being let go."

Guillaume leaned forward. "Why is that? How do you know these things?"

"I hear things, some men still come to me with news even though I no longer work at the Nor'Wester." He shrugged. "I heard that the lady's maid was caught with one of the Company clerks in a delicate situation..." Amusement glinted in his eyes. "Serves her right, going around with her nose in the air. Like she's better than the rest of us. Josie tells me the girl came from Liverpool. She'd never get a placement in a respectable house back in England, but here...she was the only one who was willing to take ship and come to this backwater. Her words, and I've heard she's regretted that decision."

"Just as well it was Josie. The man servant slithered out the back of Dutch George's when he saw me in the store, but Archie and his gang caught him before he could disappear. Lady Ashmore sent Josie around the back of the store to look for him, lucky for us. She kept our secret and told her ladyship the man was nowhere to be seen."

"Good girl, Josie." Pierre smiled. "But what of the man? He's in the cells, you said."

"He is. They put him in the same cell as Thomas Scott." He glanced toward the door leading to the prison at an uproar of voices.

"I could almost feel sorry for the bastard," Pierre said. "I imagine Scott is insulted we have put a mere servant in with what he considers gentlemen."

"So it would seem," Guillaume agreed. "Ah, here is Hugh. He'll have some news for us."

Hugh O'Lone crossed the room and joined them. "You're sure this is the man? What evidence do you have?" He held up his hand as he sank into an empty chair. "I'm not doubting you, but he is demanding we send for Lord Ashmore before he will speak. The council needs to have some grounds to hold the man. Riel is reluctant to anger or insult the English."

"Give me five minutes with him and you'll have your confession." Pierre's eyes flashed and he slammed a fist on the table making the glasses jump.

Hugh shook his head. "You know where Riel stands on violence, my friend. We need some concrete evidence."

"I have Archie's word. He was hiding in a shed near where they were murdered and saw the man come, attack my sisters, and then return. Close enough to smell the lavender on his clothes and to see him. He's identified him more than once by his clothing, we just couldn't get our hands on the man until now. Also," he pulled the silver button from his pouch, "we have this." He handed it to Hugh, the fingers of his other hand played with the gold ring, but he left it where it was.

The big man gave a low whistle. "Unless I'm mistaken that is Ashmore's crest. Where did you get this?" He handed it back to Guillaume.

"From my dead sister's hand," he replied grimly. "And Josie, who works in the Ashmore kitchen, will tell the council she was asked to replace just such a button on the man servant's coat sleeve soon after the murders took place."

"The girl will be willing to come before the council?" Hugh got to his feet.

"She is," Pierre replied before Guillaume could speak.

"I will inform the council. We need to wait though before going forward. Bruce and Riel have sent word to Lord Ashmore that his servant is accused of murder and requested his presence."

"If he refuses to come?" Pierre ran a hand over his beard.

"He will come, or he will be escourted." O'Lone shrugged. "It is his choice. I will come back when there is news." He disappeared through a different door.

"Did the man say why he murdered the women?" Pierre leaned his elbows on the table, gazed over Guillaume's head.

"He refused to say much of anything. Other than at one point he spouted the usual trash about the Mètis and their women in general." Guillaume grinned. "Then Archie kicked him in the knees."

"Good man." Pierre snorted. "Where is Archie and his gang?"

"Waiting at the cabin for me to call on him. I'm sure Fèlicitè is being regaled with tales of their conquest along with my nephews. I'm not sure Ètienne will understand much of what it means, but Alexandre will. I'm afraid it will make him hate the English more than he does. He can't understand why Ashmore refuses to come and see him. The boy knows the man is his father."

"Better off without him," Pierre declared. "What manner of man discards his wife, even if that marriage was not sanctified by the church? The number of our women who have been abandoned is huge, better we should have let the intruders all starve and freeze those first few winters."

"If we had, we would not be in the situation we are now. But how could we know the English and the powers in Upper Canada would make promises they had no intention of keeping? The Hudson's Bay Company treated us well enough before MacDonald set his sights on Rupert's Land."

A blast of cold air heralded an arrival. Miles Ashmore strode into the room, leaving his man to close the door behind him. His gaze swept over Guillaume and Pierre without any acknowledgement. He stood in the centre of the room, waiting with an imperious air for someone to attend him. Bishop Tachè disappeared through the same door O'Lone had taken and moments later returned with John Bruce.

"Bruce," Ashmore's voice was cold. "What is the meaning of this?"

"Lord Ashmore," Bruce greeted him without the bowed head Ashmore clearly expected. "If you would come with me, we can discuss this in private."

"We can discuss it here," he demanded. "Why have you called me here? I have more important things to take care of."

Bruce sighed and clasped his hands behind his back. "One of your servants has been accused of murder. We have him in custody, and he has asked for your presence."

"What manner of nonsense is this? Murder? Of whom may I ask?" Ashmore's thick brows drew together, and outrage suffused his face.

"The murder of Marguerite and Marie-Anne Mousseau. The same Marguerite Mousseau who was your wife by virtue of *à la façon du pays.*"

"This is nonsense. Just a way of embarrassing me because I chose to marry an Englishwoman. One who is married to me in the eyes of the Lord and by the rites of the church. I must insist you release my man at once."

John Bruce shook his head, a small frown creasing his forehead. "I'm afraid we cannot do as you wish. There is evidence of his involvement. If you would please come with me, we can discuss this in private." Bruce turned toward the inner door and took a few steps.

Lord Ashmore moved with him almost involuntarily. "What evidence could you possibly have. Since it is Gregory who failed to return from accompanying my wife on her shopping trip, I must assume it is he you are holding unlawfully."

"Not unlawfully. The Council of the Provisional Government holds sway, and we are within our rights to hold any who breaks the peace. I assure you, we have evidence that points to your man. A witness and a piece of physical evidence which could only have come from your household."

Lord Ashmore sniffed loudly and glared at Guillaume and Pierre before looking down his long nose at Bruce. "I assume you can produce this evidence?"

"If you would come with me, we will be happy to discuss this with you." Bruce swept an arm toward the door.

Boot heels echoing on the floorboards Ashmore allowed John Bruce to escourt him to the inner room.

Guillaume and Pierre lingered for another half an hour before Hugh O'Lone returned and crossed to their table.

"Nothing more will happen today. Riel is refusing to release the prisoner into Ashmore's keeping in spite of vigorous argument on Ashmore's part. The man will remain in the prison. May God help him survive being subjected to Scott's venom." The big man chuckled. "Go on home, go about your business. Once a date is set for the trial, I will let you know, and you will need to have your witnesses ready."

"We will be prepared. *Merci* for your help, *mon ami*." Guillaume clasped Hugh's forearm and squeezed.

"It is my pleasure. Your sisters were sweet women, they didn't deserve what happened to them. I will see you later at the saloon?" He strode back out of the room.

Pierre and Guillaume got to their feet, pulled on their mitts, and tightened their coats before stepping out into the cold and taking the long walk back to the village of Winnipeg.

Chapter Sixteen

Guillaume, Pierre, and Baptiste, along with Fèlicitè and Archie gathered in the room where a council of six men waited to hear the evidence against Lord Ashmore's servant Gregory Jones. Baptiste's wife agreed to stay with Guillaume's nephews who were too young to be present and hear the gruesome details of their mother and auntie's death.

The rustle of clothing and murmur of voices in both French and English quieted as Louis Riel and John Bruce took their places.

Gregory Jones was escourted in by two bearded Mètis men and made to stand facing the council. Bruce got to his feet to begin the proceedings after a brief prayer by Bishop Tachè. Jones had no legal representation so was forced to speak on his own behalf.

"Gregory Jones, you are charged with the murder of two Mètis women, Marguerite Mousseau and Marie-Anne Mousseau. How do you plead?" John Bruce regarded the slight figure before him.

Gregory lifted his head and glared at the men in front of him. "I have nothing to say to the likes of you."

Riel shifted in his seat but allowed Bruce to proceed. "The evidence against this man?" Bruce turned to Guillaume.

He got to his feet and addressed the six men in French. "On the night of November 28, 1869, my sisters, Marguerite and Marie-Anne Mousseau went to Lord Ashmore's house to ask assistance because one of Lord Ashmore's children born to my sister Marguerite when they were considered married according to the custom of the country was in peril. The youngest boy was gravely ill and needed medicines. My sisters did indeed get a script from Lord Ashmore for the medicine, and they made their way to Schultz's drug store, where I have it on good authority, they were given the medicines and departed. However, they never returned home and in the morning their bodies were found beaten on the street. The bodies were taken to the priest at Fort Garry to be stored until spring when the ground is thawed enough to dig their final resting place. I was granted time with them, and I found a silver button clenched in Marie-Anne's hand. This silver button." Guillaume withdrew it from his pouch and presented it to the council to examine. "As you can see it has a very distinctive marking, a coat of arms, Lord Ashmore's coat of arms to be exact."

"That can hardly be enough to accuse a man of murder." Lord Ashmore rose and spoke on behalf of his man, where just moments before he had left the man to his own defence.

One of Riel's followers moved to stand near the Englishman in case of trouble.

"There is more. As I searched for answers as to what happened to my sisters, I was approached by a young man who claimed he had seen a man attack two women on the night of the murder. He was homeless and sleeping in a shack when he was awakened by someone stealing by his hiding place. He heard the attack and then saw the same person go back the way he came. Later, he saw the accused, Gregory Jones, and identified him on numerous occasions as the man he saw that night. He is willing to tell his story if the council wishes to hear it in his own words." Guillaume glanced at Archie who sat white faced clutching Fèlicitè's hand.

"If there is need, we'll call on him. For now, please continue," Bruce instructed Guillaume.

"On further inquiry it came to light that one of the maids employed by Lord Ashmore was asked to replace a button, a button identical to the one you are holding, on Gregory Jones' coat sleeve. She is willing to speak if you wish to verify this, even though it puts her job in jeopardy." Guillaume produced the stained length of heavy wood and offered it to the council. Stepping back, he spread his arms. "That is our proof."

The accused stood rigid, trembling so hard his boots scraped on the floorboards. He turned his head toward Lord Ashmore, but his gaze fastened on Lady Ashmore.

"Do you have anything to say?" Bruce asked Jones in French.

The man shook his head, having no idea what was being asked of him.

Bruce turned to the council. "Based on the evidence before you are you ready to make a decision?"

The six men conferred, and Paul Proulx stepped forward. "We are." They retired to another room to go over the evidence and vote on a decision. Fifteen minutes, they filed back in. Proulx spoke for the other men. "We sentence this man to death by firing squad for the murder of Marguerite and Marie-Anne Mousseau."

A murmur ran through the French Half-breeds who were in attendance. Louis Riel stepped forward to explain the verdict to Jones and to those who were ignorant of the French language.

Jones' face paled to paper white, and his knees threatened to buckle. He raised his bound hands as in supplication and turned toward the Ashmores. "I only did what I was ordered to do," he shouted. "You can't kill a man for following orders. Tell them, tell them it was you who ordered me to get rid of those two troublemakers. Tell them!" Jones shrieked and fell to his knees, pointing his bound hands at Lord Ashmore. "It was him,

Lord Ashmore who told me to go and take care of the woman, get rid of them he said, after they left that night. I knew where they were headed, I followed them and when I saw which way they went I cut through the empty lots and waited until they came. I had no choice, I had to do it."

A Mètis guard hauled Jones to his feet. Bruce and Riel turned to Lord Ashmore.

"Is this true? Did you order your servant to murder the two women?" Riel's intense gaze bored into the Englishman, whose wife shrank back behind him, her eyes on Gregory Jones.

"Of course, I did no such thing. The man is clearly lying to save himself. I saw Marguerite that night and I gave her a script for medicine for the boy. Why would I then send my man out to murder her before she could take it home to the child? This makes no sense."

"It was you...it was you," Jones sobbed, staring at Lord Ashmore.

Riel and Bruce put their heads together to confer. Guillaume clenched his hands on his thighs, his leg bouncing with the urge to leap to his feet and beat both men into a pulp. His instincts had been right, even though the evidence all pointed to the servant, his gut told him all along it was Ashmore who was behind it. Beside him, Pierre was being restrained by Baptiste who had a firm grasp on him. Archie sat wide-eyed and trembling while Fèlicitè murmured in his ear with tears on her cheeks. An angry buzz filled the room, hostile eyes on the tall Englishman in his fine clothing. Lady Ashmore hovered behind him. Guillaume noticed in an abstracted way that her gaze was still fixed on Gregory Jones.

Bruce and Riel separated, and Bruce addressed the accused. "To clarify for the council, you are now accusing your employer, Lord Ashmore, of ordering you to carry out the murder of the two women. Is that correct?"

"Yes, yes, it was him. Lord Ashmore who ordered me to get rid of the women." He straightened up and glared at the council and the others gathered. "They were nothing to me and there's lots of whores around, I figured who was going to miss those two?"

Guillaume and Pierre both bolted to their feet, hands on the hilts of their knives. Guillaume wished for his gun, his vision blurred with a wash of red, the only clear image was Gregory Jones. Baptiste hauled Pierre out of the room struggling and shouting curses at both Englishmen. Fèlicitè laid a hand on Guillaume's arm and tugged him back into his seat.

Four armed Mètis soldiers surrounded Lord and Lady Ashmore, preventing either of them from slipping away. Charlotte Ashmore looked down her aristocratic nose at them and sniffed in disgust, twitching her skirts so they didn't touch any of them.

Bruce nodded at Riel. "Take Lord Ashmore into custody, he is charged with ordering the murder of Marguerite and Marie-Anne Mousseau," Riel ordered.

"This is insanity! I am a British Lord, and you have no jurisdiction over me. Unhand me!" Ashmore's face flushed above the stark white of his neckcloth.

"We have every right. The Provisional Government is in charge, not your British monarch or MacDonald in Upper Canada," Bruce stated.

"I'm free to go then," Jones announced. "You have your culprit, set me free."

The council, along with Bruce and Riel, regarded him in astonishment.

"Your sentence stands. It was by your hand the two women were murdered." Riel nodded at the men flanking Jones. "Take him back to the cell while we deal with this development."

Jones took two steps toward the Ashmores, arms extended. "Save me, tell them." He broke into tears as the soldiers half dragged him toward the door to the cells. "Tell them." His protestations faded as the door closed behind the men.

"Bring his Lordship to the front," Bruce instructed two of the soldiers flanking Lord Ashmore.

Ashmore shook off their hands in an imperious gesture and stalked to the front to regard the council. Lady Ashmore attempted to slip back into the crowd in the direction of the outer door. With a glance, Riel instructed the two soldiers remaining beside her to keep her in place.

"Surely you know this is nonsense," Lord Ashmore began.

"Miles, make them let me go home. I feel faint," Lady Ashmore's voice interrupted him.

He glanced in her direction. "My wife is feeling ill, kindly permit her to return home."

Bruce met Riel's gaze across the room and nodded briefly. "She stays for now," Riel said. He gestured to one of the men with her to fetch a chair so she could sit. Charlotte Ashmore plumped herself onto the chair and glared at Riel. Crossing her hand primly in her lap, she pointedly ignored those around her. Her gaze fell on Josie, huddled beside Fèlicitè and Archie. Rage and fury contorted her features for a moment, gone almost before Guillaume saw it. Then her features returned to the smooth blank mask of superiority.

Ashmore shook his head in disgust. "As you wish. I'm sure we can bring this travesty to a quick close and I can escourt my wife home."

"I am not as sure of that as you seem to be," Lèpine, who acting as judge, informed him. "Serious accusations have been brought against you by one of your own people."

"Who is clearly trying to save his own skin." Ashmore's polished boots reflected the light as he shifted weight from one foot to the other, betraying his agitation.

"Tell us your version please. If I recall correctly, you were one of the first people to arrive when the women were found," one of the council addressed him.

"I was. One of the trappers heading to the Company store raised the alarm and I came to find out what was wrong. Think about it man, if I had anything to do with their deaths do you think I would rush right over there?"

"You might well have if only to deflect any suspicion away from yourself," another council member speculated.

"This is insanity." Ashmore ground his teeth. "Bring Jones back out here and let us get to the bottom of this. It is his word against mine and all your evidence points toward him. Clearly, he is hoping to use me as a scapegoat and somehow wriggle out of the fact he murdered two women. I do not see how I can be held responsible for his actions when I knew nothing of them before this." Ashmore spoke confidently, but a bead of sweat rolled down his face in front of his ear.

Riel crossed over to where Bruce was in conference with Lèpine. Guillaume strained to catch snatches of the conversation when the men's voices raised. His heart twisted in his chest, the English bastard was going to go free, when every bone in Guillaume's body was positive the servant was correct, and

Ashmore ordered him to murder the women. He spared a glance at Lady Ashmore, surprising a smug look of victory on her face, a sly smile tilting her lips. She raised her eyes for a moment and caught his gaze before a cold mask slid over her features. What a strange woman, she was. All holier than thou and acting as if she were above even the other Englishwomen in the village and yet her face betrayed her baser emotions when she wasn't being careful. He could almost pity Ashmore for having to live with her. Motion near the door to the cells brought his attention back to the front of the room.

Gregory Jones was led back into the room, his face blotched and red, hair awry. He shrank away from the expression on Lord Ashmore's face when he was made to stand close to him. Ashmore glared down at the man. Jones shuffled as far away from him as the guards would allow. Lèpine nodded for John Bruce to take command of the situation.

"Mister Jones," he spoke in English this time, "what proof do you have that Lord Ashmore forced you to murder the two women, other than your own words?"

Jones flicked his gaze to Bruce and swallowed with an audible gulp. "How can I have proof? He told me, there wasn't anything in writing, no one heard him, he made sure of that…I swear on my mother's grave I'm telling you the truth."

Guillaume leaned forward; hands clasped hard between his knees. His eyes narrowed when he noticed Jones sending covert glances toward where Lady Ashmore sat regally erect at the side of the room. *Interesting, does he think she will come to his rescue? I wonder what she knows about all this.* Lord Ashmore's explosion of disgust brought his attention back to the proceedings.

"Will you take the word of a disgruntled servant over mine?" Ashmore stared down the council, each man in turn.

Riel turned to Bishop Tachè. "Bishop, if you would assist?"

"Of course," Tachè responded. "How may I be of service?"

Riel approached Gregory Jones. "Are you willing to swear on the Holy Bible that what you say is the truth?"

Jones nodded, his unbound hair falling across his eyes. He turned his imploring gaze on Lady Ashmore before replying to Riel. "Yes, yes. I am willing."

"Bishop Tachè, if you would be so kind." Riel called the bishop forward.

Pulling a Bible from his robes Bishop Tachè approached Jones. He held the book out and instructed Jones to place his right hand on the cover.

"Do you swear that you speak the truth to this council?"

"Yes," Jones voice quavered but was audible to all in the room.

"Do you swear that it was on Lord Ashmore's implicit orders that you committed the serious crime of murder?" Tachè kept his eyes on the man as he spoke.

Sweat rolled down the prisoner's face and his hand shook on the cover of the Bible. "Yes, I only did it because I couldn't lose my job, I have nowhere else to go." He glanced sideways at the tall man beside him. "He forced me to do it, threatened to turn me out if I didn't."

"Lies, he speaks lies," Ashmore ground the words out. "I gave no such order, and I never had any conversation with this man regarding any harm coming to the Mousseau sisters." He made a move toward his former servant and was restrained by two guards. He regained his composure and shook off their hands before turning to address the council. "This man is lying and endangering his soul by doing so with his hand on the Bible. I have never wished Marguerite or Marie-Anne any harm and I am distressed that they are with God now instead of walking among us as they should be. I offer you my word as a gentleman that I had no part in this gruesome affair."

Bishop Tachè tucked the Bible back in his robes and returned to the edge of the room beside Riel. The two men conversed in voices too low for Guillaume to make out anything. Finally, Riel moved to speak with Bruce, nodding toward the two men in custody and then the council. Bruce broke off the conversation and approached Lèpine.

"The council has heard the evidence and had some time to consider it. Are you ready to vote in this matter?" Bruce stood beside Lèpine's desk.

Lèpine rose and the council got to their feet as well. "We will go and make a decision and be back as soon as possible." He led the other five men into a small separate room.

Jones and Lord Ashmore stayed where they were surrounded by the four guards. Ashmore flicked dust from his sleeves and pointedly ignored the man beside him. Again, Jones turned a bit so he could scan the people gathered, his gaze flicking to Lady Ashmore more than once.

Guillaume clenched his teeth. The waiting was almost worse than the not knowing who to blame for his sisters' deaths. Archie sat hunched beside him, chewing on a thumb nail. Fèlicitè reached over and laid a hand on Guillaume's arm in support. He covered it with his own drawing comfort from the contact. Finally, the creak of floorboards followed by the squeak of the door heralded the return of the council.

Lèpine stood in front of the desk, flanked by the other members of the council, and swept his gaze over the gathering before addressing the two men in front of him.

"We have voted, and as appointed judge, I have made a decision regarding the matter before us. We find Gregory Jones guilty of murder, by his own admission. His employer's orders notwithstanding, he did plan and carry out the murders of Marguerite and Marie-Anne Mousseau. The verdict of death by firing squad stands." He waited for the murmurs in the room to subside. "Lord Ashmore is another matter, we have the testimony of the accused, sworn on the Holy Bible by Bishop Tachè, and although there is no other evidence we must take that testimony seriously, as we did when we voted. The council finds Lord Ashmore guilty of conspiring in the murders of Marguerite and Marie-Anne Mousseau." He turned to the council. Pierre Delorme had moved that the death sentence be invoked and Xavier Pageè seconded it. It wasn't a unanimous vote by the other members but Lèpine ruled that the vote was four to two and so the movement stood.

The room erupted in an uproar. Ashmore shouting at the top of his lungs while Jones crumpled to the floor in a heap. Lady Ashmore attempted to break through the guards to reach her husband. Guillaume gripped Fèlicitè's hand, triumph that his sisters would be avenged tempered by the knowledge he would have to tell his nephews they wouldn't see their papa again.

"Return them to the cells," Riel ordered in an attempt to regain control of the room.

The guards dragged Jones to his feet while two large soldiers gripped Ashmore by the arms, forcing him to move toward the door to the cells while he struggled against them.

"Wait! Stop!" A high female voice rose over the cacophony of the room. "Wait! I have something to say." A young woman in a maid uniform forced her way through the crowd.

"What are you doing? You can't save him." Lady Ashmore hissed as the woman tried to pass her. She gripped the younger woman's arm.

"Telling the truth." She ripped her arm free of Lady Ashmore's grip.

"Hold," Lèpine ordered. "What is the meaning of this interruption, do you have something to add to these proceedings?"

The young woman came to a halt in front of Lèpine's desk, shoving her disheveled hair back from her face, gasping to catch her breath. "Yes. I need to speak the truth."

"Who are you?" Louis Riel moved to stand at Lèpine's right shoulder behind the desk.

"Amelia Adams, sir. I'm Lady Ashmore's maid." She cast a frantic glance at the woman in question who was being restrained in her seat by one of the soldiers.

"What is it you wish to tell us," John Bruce addressed her. "You are too late at any rate as the sentence has been passed."

"You can't execute an innocent man," she protested.

"There are two men charged and found guilty. Which of them do you claim is innocent and what is your proof?"

Amelia's gaze fixed on the tall figure of the British lord. "Like I said, I'm Lady Ashmore's maid, so I spend a lot of time in her rooms and with her, helping her dress and running errands for her. So sometimes I hear things I'm not supposed to." She turned her eyes to Riel. "You know how some people treat servants like we are part of the furniture and have no ears or a brain of our own. I heard things and I saw things I should not have." She paused and swallowed, twisting her hands in her skirts, shoulders vibrating so the cloth of her cloak rustled in the now silent room.

"What things would those be? The things you know and should not?" Bruce prompted her.

"Amelia, I beg you, be silent," Jones beseeched her.

She raised her head. "I can't Gregory, I can't."

Lèpine rapped his fist on the desk. "Say what you wish to say or sit down. You are wasting our time."

The young woman straightened her shoulders and looked Lèpine in the eye. "Lord Ashmore has nothing to do with the murders of those poor women. I was still on duty the night they came to the door asking for help from his Lordship. Gregory answered the door just as I was coming down the stairs on the way to the kitchen to get the warming pans for the beds and prepare the tea her Ladyship likes before turning in, so I heard everything." She sent a quick smile toward Lord Ashmore, who stood dumbfounded staring at her. "Lady Ashmore instructed Gregory to send them away, claimed her husband had no sons, even though we all know he does. But then his Lordship heard the voices and came to the door. She tried to block him from seeing who was there, but one of the women, I think she said her name was Marguerite called to him and he spoke with her. Agreed to write a note for the doctor to give her the medicine she needed for her child. I heard her Ladyship tell him he needed to do something about her. It upset her and embarrassed her among the other ladies of the community."

"How does this prove that either man is innocent of what they are charged with?" Riel fixed her with his dark compelling gaze.

"After I took the warming pans upstairs, I went back to the kitchen to get the tea tray. When I went into the sitting room Lady Ashmore was with Gregory. They ignored me and so I set the tray down and started to leave, Lord Ashmore wasn't in the room at the time. I heard Lady Ashmore tell Gregory he needed to hurry and fetch her what she asked for. She insisted it must be now or it would be too late. She often asked him to do things which seemed odd to me, I once caught him coming out of her bed chamber well past midnight.”

A shriek of outrage from Lady Ashmore interrupted her. “Why are you telling such lies?” She dabbed at her eyes with a dainty hanky.

“It’s the God’s honest truth.” Amelia firmed her chin. “I returned to the kitchen to be sure Cook and the kitchen maid had things in order for the morning, then Gregory came through on his way out. I asked him where he was going, but he kept his head down, his face hidden by a hat, just grunted at me. Which, considering it was pretty late and stormy, seemed more than odd. I mean nothing would be open except the saloons and perhaps Doctor Schultz’s. Josie, the kitchen maid, had already left so I stayed to help Cook with a few things. Gregory, or who I assumed was Gregory, came back about ha’past the hour out of breath with his coat torn and missing a button.” She gulped and blinked. “There was blood on the coat and on his hands, blood spattered all over the front and arm of the coat. He took off the hat and I swear I thought me heart would jump out of me throat. It wasn’t Gregory at all.” She stopped and swallowed hard, trembling so her skirts rustled against the rough floor.

“What do you mean it wasn’t Gregory? Who else could it be?” Lèpine demanded.

I tell you, Cook was as surprised as meself. You could have knocked us both over with a feather." She paused and drew a shaky breath. "When he took off the hat, it wasn't who I thought it was, it was... Lady Ashmore."

"You lying bitch!" Charlotte Ashmore sprang to her feet, fingers curled like claws, and lurched toward Amelia. She was restrained by the two men at her side. "How dare you accuse me of dressing like a *man*?"

A wave of whispers and gasps ran through the room. Guillaume started to rise and was restrained by Fèlicitè.

"It was, it was Lady Ashmore. Cool as could be, she stripped off the coat and handed it to Cook. Gregory came into the kitchen right then, he was shaking and white-faced. He said, 'Did you do it?' And Lady Ashmore nodded. 'All taken care of,' she said. Then she asked where Lord Ashmore was. Gregory told her he was upstairs sleeping, the stuff she'd given him in his tea worked like a charm. He'd never know she'd been gone. She took the dressing gown Gregory had in his hands and stepped into the pantry. When she came out with the robe wrapped around her, she threw the blood-stained shirt into the fire and made sure it burned up. Cook was soaking the coat in cold water. I was trying to slip out the door without being noticed. But Lady Ashmore grabbed my arm and hissed at me. Made me promise not to say anything to anyone, especially Lord Ashmore. Made Cook promise too. Threatened to turn me out with no references if I said a word. I was scared to death, I was.

"What happened after that?" Lèpine leaned forward on his elbows, his gaze flicking from Lord Ashmore to his wife before meeting Bruce's.

"She told Cook to have Josie replace the button on the sleeve of the coat, she said she must have snagged it on a bush on her way back. Then she left the kitchen and went upstairs. To bed, I suppose. Gregory gathered up his trousers and boots and picked up the hat that she'd borrowed. He stood in the middle of the kitchen with them clutched to his chest and started to cry. He kept whispering, 'Oh Charlotte, what have you done, what have you done?' I'd never heard him call Lady Ashmore by her given name before. But I swear on my mother's grave Lord Ashmore had nothing to do with any of it. Cook and I, we had no idea right then what she'd been about, but with all that blood..." Amelia's voice trailed off and she sent a terrified glance toward Charlotte Ashmore who was livid with rage.

"Cook asked me to bring in some wood for the morning. I went to fetch it and picked up a good-sized piece lying beside the pile...it was wet and when I wiped my hand on my skirts, I realized it was blood. After what I just saw in the kitchen, I was too scared to even think straight. I added the wood to my pile and as soon as I got back inside, I threw it on the fire. When I heard the news the next morning about those poor women, I knew, just knew, that's what she'd been about the night before. Later that day, she accused me of stealing her gold signet ring, but I didn't. Josie told me sometime later that Mister Mousseau had found a gold ring here his sisters were murdered."

Guillaume stood and pulled the signet ring from his pouch. "I have the ring here. Do you recognize it?" He passed it to Lord Ashmore who clutched it in his hand.

"Charlotte? That is the ring you said your maid stole..." Lord Ashmore stared at his wife, aghast. "Surely not, Charlotte?"

Charlotte Ashmore surged to her feet, shaking off the two guards and fisting her hands on her hips she glared at him, vibrating with fury. "For God's sake Miles, what was I to do? It was bad enough when everyone who matters knew you had illegitimate offspring with that savage, but to have her come to my door, stand on my doorstep and demand to speak with you...I beseech you, what else was I supposed to do?" Her gaze swept the room, glancing over Guillaume as her lip lifted in distain. "So, yes, I borrowed your man servant's clothes and took care of it as he didn't have the guts to do it for me. I couldn't imagine anyone would miss a couple of stinking savages. I did the community a service. You should be thanking me, and him." She tipped her head toward Gregory Jones.

"Oh, Charlotte, how could you?" Miles Ashmore whispered.

Lady Ashmore took a step toward her husband but was restrained by the two guards at her side, another blocking the door. "How could I not? Her existence, and all those like her, is an insult to good breeding and civility. You were not willing to address the situation and it just could not continue. It could not. I have my pride, you know. Did you even think about how embarrassing it was for me to see acquaintances whisper behind their hands about your *other family*, and gossip about the fact you have given *me* no children? I took care of things as you would not. Surely, I cannot be blamed for protecting my honour?"

"Charlotte," Lord Ashmore spread his hands, "Look where you are, to whom you are speaking…"

She raised her chin in defiance. "I did nothing wrong. I was only protecting what is mine by right." She glared at Amelia who still stood by Lèpine's desk, eyes narrowed and fury twisting her delicate features. "You," she pointed a shaking finger, "you will vacate my premises immediately and you can expect no references from me. No one will hire you after this betrayal."

Amelia lifted her chin. "I would rather starve than work a moment longer for you." She turned and moved toward the door.

"Please remain until we agree you can leave." Bruce's voice halted her.

Nodding, she moved to stand beside Josie behind Guillaume and Archie.

The council of six men conferred with John Bruce and Louis Riel with much agitated movement of hands and muttering. Finally, Baptise Lèpine addressed the gathering.

"Given the evidence provided by the young woman, and Lady Ashmore's own admission, we absolve Lord Ashmore of any wrongdoing, other than perhaps his choice of a wife. Gregory Jones remains in custody as an accessory to murder, we will rethink our decision regarding his fate in the light of the new evidence." He regarded Lady Ashmore with some distaste. "Lady Ashmore will be held responsible for her part in this tragedy. We are reluctant to hold her in the cells, but as both John Schultz and Charles Mair both have their wives beside them, she will not be the only woman there. Take her and put her with the other women. Return Jones to his cell for the moment."

Lord Ashmore approached the council and spoke with Lèpine, Bruce, and Riel. Guillaume clenched his fists in frustration. If the man somehow secured his wife's freedom, there would be retribution. The woman was a self-confessed murderer.

Archie stared after Lady Ashmore as she was escourted from the room. "It was her, all along. It was her," he whispered, shaking his head. "I never would'a guessed."

"Nor would I," Guillaume assured him. He turned and caught Fèlicitè's eye. "I know I should not, but I wish that woman dead by my hand."

Fèlicitè laid a hand on his arm. "To do so would jeopardize your eternal soul, that woman is not worth the cost of your soul." She shook her head. "Jealousy will make a person do awful things. Hate and love are like two sides of the same coin."

Guillaume got to his feet as the room emptied. Fèlicitè and Archie followed him out into the cold where they joined Baptiste and Pierre who were waiting outside.

"Is it true, what they said? It was Ashmore's wife who did it?" Pierre grabbed Guillaume's arm.

"Oui, by her own admission. Her maid burst in and accused her and then she confessed everything."

Pierre moved off a few paces, scrubbing his face and muttering to himself. Fèlicitè moved to speak softly with him.

"Who would ever have thought the Englishwoman was capable of such a thing," Baptiste said.

"I knew she resented the children and Marguerite, but never did I imagine anything like this." Guillaume turned toward his cabin, Fèlicitè and Archie walking between him and Baptiste. Pierre strode off toward O'Lone's saloon. Archie wore a dumbfounded expression on his thin face. He let Fèlicitè keep hold of his hand.

"How could someone so beautiful be so cruel?" he asked.

"Ah, *mon ami*. Beauty is only on the surface, to find true beauty one must look inside, below the surface." Baptiste bestowed an adoring glance at his daughter.

Following his gaze, Archie smiled, pulling his hand free, he put his arm around Fèlicitè's waist. "You are right, Baptiste." He looked up at the woman at his side. "You are more beautiful than any Englishwoman," he told Fèlicitè.

She smiled at him and dropped a kiss on his cheek, surprised at how much the boy had grown in the little time she'd known him. Guillaume's gaze caught on hers, she twitched the corner of her mouth in a half-smile, the dimple in her cheek flashing.

Guillaume almost missed his footing before he returned his attention to where his feet were taking him.

Chapter Seventeen

"What will happen now? What did they decide?" Fèlicitè asked when Guillaume returned from the village two days later.

Guillaume sank into the chair by the fire and tipped his head back. "The council has voted to change Jones' death sentence to banishment from the country. From what was Rupert's Land and the Northwest. He is being escourted back to Upper Canada."

"What about Lady Ashmore?" Archie broke in. "Are they going to put her in front of the firing squad? I want to watch that."

"No, you don't." Guillaume fixed him with a stern gaze. "The taking of a human life is not something to be celebrated, no matter how justified you might feel."

"Are they really thinking about doing that? The firing squad, I mean." Fèlicitè came and sat in the opposite chair, handing him a mug of tea.

"*Non*, the men have no stomach for that at the best of times...and a woman...*non*. Riel is against such violence at any rate, not to mention the uproar it would cause in the east if we were to execute an Englishwoman.

"What will happen to her? Surely, she can't be allowed to keep living here as if nothing happened?" Fèlicitè clenched her fists in her lap.

"The last I heard the council was debating banishing Lady Ashmore from the country as well. When I left Riel, Bruce and Lord Ashmore were deep in conversation, I imagine about what was going to happen in that regard."

He was interrupted by a bang on the door. Shooting a troubled glance at Fèlicitè, he nodded for her to take the two young boys behind the curtain that separated the sleeping area from the main cabin. Once they disappeared, he moved to the door. Archie a step behind him. He removed the bar as another rap sounded on the wood.

"Guillaume." Lord Ashmore stood in the doorway.

"Ashmore," Guillaume replied. "What do you want here?" He made no move to invite the man over the doorstep.

The Englishman cleared his throat. "I have news that I believe you will be interested in." He paused. "And I would like to see the boys, if you would permit it."

Archie leaped between the two men before Guillaume was aware of his intention. "You got no right to see my brothers. Go on, git out of here!" Archie threw his thin frame against the taller man attempting to push him out of the doorway.

“Archie,” Guillaume warned. He took the young man by the shoulders and set him behind him. “What do you really want?” he addressed Ashmore.

“A number of things that would best be discussed out of the cold.” Ashmore quirked an eyebrow and tipped his head toward the interior. “Things to your benefit, I might add.”

Guillaume debated with himself for a moment. One part of him was curious to hear what the man had to say, the larger part of him wanted to plant a fist in the man’s face and pound him into the dirt. Heaving a sigh, he stepped back and allowed the Englishman to enter, ignoring Archie’s hiss of indignation.

Ashmore surveyed the small cabin, standing somewhat awkwardly in the middle of the floor. Guillaume refrained from offering him a seat.

“Speak what it is you have to say,” he said.

The Englishman nodded, a weary expression crossing his face. “Lady Ashmore’s fate has been decided. I have agreed to take her back to England and agreed she will never set foot in Canada or Winnipeg and its environs again.”

“You’re not stayin’ married to her, are you? She’s a murderer!” Archie marched up to Ashmore’s boot tips. “What kinda man are you?” Disgust written plain on his young face.

"What I do with my wife upon our return to England is none of your concern, young man." He returned his attention to Guillaume. "I will make sure she will cause no harm to anyone again. There are places in London and the countryside for women who suffer from hysteria. Lady Ashmore will be taken to such a place where she will stay until the end of her days." He thrust his hand forward. "My word on it."

Frowning, Guillaume hesitated and then clasped the offered hand.

"You must believe me. I never wished any harm to come to either of your sisters. I had no idea Charlotte was so volatile or indeed capable of such behaviour. I assured Marguerite I would provide for the boys and so I will. That is in part of why I am here." He thrust a hand into the pocket of his jacket and pulled out a crisp envelope. "This should help with the boys' upkeep and I am happy to offer to bring them to London, should they ever wish it, and enroll them in the best schools. Their heritage might make it difficult for them in English society, but the choice is there if they wish to pursue it." He handed the envelope to Guillaume.

He opened it, thumbing through the papers inside. Some bank notes, some land scripts met his gaze. "I will see this is put aside for my nephews." He nodded his thanks.

"There is also this." Ashmore passed him a small leather purse that sat heavy in Guillaume's palm.

The coins inside clinked softly as he tucked the purse in his pouch. "It is good of you to think of providing for them," he said with some reluctance.

"Could I see them, please. To say goodbye? I plan to leave in the morning, going south to St. Cloud and then east from there. The roads are much better to the south and travel will be easier."

"Papa?" Alexandre's high-pitched voice came from behind the curtain. "Papa? Is that you at last?"

Ashmore looked to Guillaume who nodded and stepped away, pulling a hissing Archie with him.

"Yes, Alex, it is me. I have missed you." Ashmore knelt and was almost bowled over by the child who bolted across the floor and threw himself into the man's arms. He gathered the boy close, moisture shining on his cheeks.

Fèlicitè emerged from behind the curtain with Ètienne clutching her skirts. She gave him a tiny push toward his father, her eyes on Guillaume.

"Come and see Papa," Alexandre urged his brother. He reached back with one hand and pulled Ètienne forward.

"Look how you've grown! Such fine young men you are becoming. I am so proud of both of you." Ashmore put out an arm toward the youngest boy. Ètienne shrank back but allowed him to stroke his hair. "It's been too long since I visited you, Ètienne. I must seem a stranger to you."

"You are our papa," Alexandre declared, gripping his hand tightly. "*Maman* said we were to always respect you. That you loved us, but that now you had a new family, and we must not bother you." He tipped his head back. "Why did you need a new family when you already had us?"

"Your *maman* was correct. I do love you both. Right now, I cannot imagine why I felt I needed a different family. I cannot explain how foolish I have been. But you must listen to me very carefully. I am going away, back to England. Across the ocean. I have left money with your uncle so you will be well taken care of. If you should ever decide you wish to come to England, you have only to contact me. Your uncle has the address you would write to."

"Why are you going away? Can't we come with you?" Alexandre wrapped himself around the Englishman's booted leg. Ètienne stared up at him, wiping a hand across his nose.

"I have business that I must attend to. If it were my choice I would stay, but it is not. Try to understand. I will write to you often, if that meets with your uncle's approval. But

I must go." He stood up and took Alexandre's face in his hands, kissing both cheeks. He managed to drop a kiss on Ètienne's head before the youngster retreated back to the safety of Fèlicitè's skirts.

He straightened and turned to Guillaume, one hand resting on Alexandre's shoulder. "My thanks for allowing me to say farewell to my sons. If you ever have need of anything you have only to ask." With a last anguished look at the two little boys, Ashmore stepped out the door.

Archie rushed to close it behind him and slide the bar into place. "Bastard," he muttered.

"Archie!" Fèlicitè warned. "What have I told you about using that kind of language."

Guillaume laughed and tousled the young man's hair. "Maybe not so much of a bastard as I once thought. Now that all this is settled, I must go find Pierre and see that he knows about the council's decision. Then I need to speak with Baptiste about something important." His gaze was on Fèlicitè, something warm and promising in his dark eyes.

"I will be here when you return," she promised.

The End

Arabella Dreams ~ Book Two

Co-Authored with Pat Dale
The Last Cowboy
Henrietta's Heart
The Teddy Dialogues
She's Driving Me Crazy

Historical Horror
By N.M. Bell
No Absolution

Bibliography

Riel, A life of Revolution Maggie Siggins Harper Collins1942 0-00-215792-6

Canadian Wilds Martin Hunter 1907 Create Space Publication 2013 978-1494333874

Reporting the Resistance A Begg and J Hargrave 1869-1870 edited by JM Bumstead University of Manitoba Press 0-88755-675-22003

The Company The Rise and Fall of the Hudson's Bay Empire Stephen R Bown Penguin Random House Canada/Anchor Canada 2020 9780385694094

https://www.thecanadianencyclopedia.ca/en/article/red-river-rebellion
http://www.mhs.mb.ca/docs/transactions/3/norwester.shtml
For those interested the name Guilluame is pronounced Gee-ume - the double ll pronounced as a 'y'

Nancy M Bell has publishing credits in poetry, fiction, and non-fiction. Nancy has presented at the Surrey International Writers Conference, When Words Collide, and the Writers Guild of Alberta Conference. Nancy enjoys working with new and emerging as well as seasoned authors providing editing and support to her fellow authors. She loves writing fiction and poetry and following wherever her muse takes her.

She is at https://bookswelove.net/bell-nancy/
Please visit her webpage
http://www.nancymbell.ca
You can find her on Facebook at
http://facebook.com/NancyMBell